Eggs over Evie

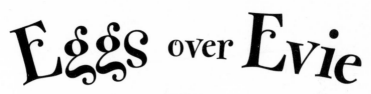

Eggs over Evie

Alison Jackson

illustrated by

Tuesday Mourning

Christy Ottaviano Books

Henry Holt and Company · New York

J-Fiction

Henry Holt and Company, LLC
Publishers since 1866
175 Fifth Avenue
New York, New York 10010
www.HenryHoltKids.com

Library of Congress Cataloging-in-Publication Data
Jackson, Alison.
Eggs over Evie / Alison Jackson ; illustrated by Tuesday Mourning. — 1st ed.
p.   cm.
"Christy Ottaviano Books."
Includes bibliographical references (p.   ).
Summary: Evie feels unsettled and sad after her parents divorce, her father
remarries and takes the family dog, and his new wife becomes pregnant, but a
cooking class and helping the elderly lady next door with her cat give Evie a
way to cope with the changes in her life. Includes recipes.
ISBN 978-0-8050-8294-4
[1. Cookery—Fiction. 2. Divorce—Fiction. 3. Stepfamilies—Fiction. 4. Pets—
Fiction.] I. Mourning, Tuesday, ill. II. Title.
PZ7.J13217Eg 2010   [Fic]—dc22   2009050762

First Edition—2010 / Designed by Véronique Lefèvre Sweet
Printed in October 2010 in the United States of America by
R. R. Donnelley & Sons Company, Harrisonburg, Virginia

1 3 5 7 9 10 8 6 4 2

For all the cooks in my family,
especially Sharon and Pam
Bon appétit!

Contents

CHAPTER 1

Delineation

"There is fabulous cooking, good cooking, mediocre cooking, and bad cooking."
—James Beard

I like to cook early in the morning. No one's around to distract me. Nobody's telling me what ingredients to add or leave out. Time doesn't exist. I measure, I pour, I beat, I blend. My mind is uncluttered.

And this morning was no exception. I knew that by noon it would be too hot to cook. Sweat already tickled the hairs on my neck, running down the insides of my arms as I whipped up my latest culinary masterpiece. The last time I'd tried making this particular soufflé, it caved in like a crater on the moon.

But I knew now what I had done wrong. Soufflés depend on eggs and time. Not one second should be wasted between the beating of the whites and the opening of the oven door. A sudden draft might be deadly.

Well—no danger of that today, I thought. *Any* draft, sudden or not, would be a welcome change. Mom had told me this heat wave might go down in the record books as the hottest in Clermont Lake's history. And she was probably right. But hot was hot. Especially when your mother was trying to save money on electricity by turning off the air-conditioning.

I'd been hanging around the house since school let out for the summer, "making a mess in the kitchen" (her words, not mine) and being slovenly in general. Chocolate chip cookies with pecans and coconut were my specialty, but I'd baked enough of those in the past few days to fill a moving van. And, to tell you the truth, I was moping a little too. I was bored and hot, nearly as deflated as last week's soufflé disaster. And I missed my dog.

Mousse is a big fat mutt of an animal, sort of a mix between a chubby retriever and a beagle, with some Great Dane thrown in to scare people. Dad was the one who named him. He said that if you let that dog loose during hunting season, someone might mistake him for a moose and try to shoot him. Mousse. A cooking term, naturally.

My father is David Carson, the renowned celebrity chef. He writes cookbooks for a living, in addition to a syndicated newspaper food column called "Carson's Cuisine." He also hosts a weekly television show on the local food channel, educating all of Clermont Lake's early risers on the mysteries of how to separate eggs or grate lemon peels. My dad loves to cook, just like I do. The big difference is . . . he's really good at it. Another difference is . . . he doesn't do any of his cooking in our house anymore.

Dad moved out about a year ago to live in a high-rise condominium on the other side of the lake. A trial separation was what he and Mom called it. Yeah, right. He was dating his young editor, and everyone knew it. Mom in particular. I mean, how could she not know? Long before Dad announced his departure, it was always "Angie" this and "Angie" that. And, oh, guess who called me the other day? And . . . do you know who *happened* to be in Toronto when I was speaking at that cooking symposium? More persistent than the flu. That was Angie.

And now Dad was living with her. Married to her, actually. With a baby on the way. But that wasn't even the worst of it. He'd taken Mousse with him. Our dog's abduction was all part of the "separation agreement," although I'd never *agreed* to any of it. Dad insisted that if Mom got custody of me, then he should get custody of Mousse. It was only fair, he argued. Meaning his thirteen-year-old daughter was a fair trade for a dog? Even a stupendously smart and wonderful dog, like Mousse.

And what about Mom? She'd given up a music career in New York. Now she taught piano to a bunch of tone-deaf kids whose mothers had read somewhere that studying music would elevate their child's IQ. Well, from the noises I heard coming out of our music room every afternoon, those IQs needed more help than my mom could ever give them.

This is not to say that I could play the piano any better. I was also tone deaf. Something else I'd inherited from my father. But as far as I knew, my IQ was okay. I took a career aptitude test in middle school last year and was told I would perform well in sales or animal care. Not a single word about cooking.

That pretty much wiped out my future dreams of Parisian culinary schools, so Mom came to the rescue. She enrolled me in a teen cooking class at the local rec center this summer. And, to make the testing people happy, I pinned up posters around the neighborhood advertising my pet-sitting services: EVIE CARSON: PET-SITTER, PET-WALKER, AND PART-TIME CHEF.

Only one customer called me up. Mrs. Hamilton from next door. That figured. I'd already been feeding her mangy cat for two years, ever since Mrs. Hamilton fell and broke her hip. For a while, the poor woman couldn't walk without wheels attached to her. But she was doing a lot better now. I mostly went over to try out my new recipes on her, and to search for Millie, the fugitive cat who was always sneaking out of the house.

Mrs. H complained about that cat night and day. And the woman hated everything I made for her, though I think she enjoyed the attention. Once I caught her slipping Millie one of my Swedish meatballs, but she denied it, as if I'd insulted her or something. Right. Like I *wasn't* insulted? Those meatballs were one of Dad's specialties. Of course, I found out later that I'd accidentally added baking soda to the recipe, instead of salt. Still, Millie ate it, so my meatballs couldn't have been that awful.

I was thinking of taking my soufflé next door later this morning, if the whole thing didn't cave in like Mount Vesuvius. Or I could share it with Mom, if she woke up in the next hour or so.

I glanced at the wall clock over the refrigerator. Ten o'clock. Why wasn't she out of bed yet? Then I heard her laughing. Mom was in the music room, talking on the phone. And I couldn't help thinking that it was good to hear her laugh. She used to do that all the time, especially when Dad made breakfast for us. Mom and I would always gag and cough, like the food was really terrible, and then he'd pretend to be offended.

Enough of that. Dad wasn't here. He was across the lake, cooking breakfast for his pregnant wife and serving the scraps to my dog!

Mom walked into the kitchen, sniffing the air.

"Soufflé again?" she said with a smile.

"New and improved," I answered. "I promise."

Mom poured herself a cup of coffee and sat at the table, opening the newspaper. We both knew that this was Saturday, the day when Dad's food column appeared in part four. But she made quite a show of avoiding that section.

I rummaged around in the fridge for some orange juice and gave the carton a hefty shake. Then I filled a glass and sat down next to her.

"Doing anything special today?" Mom asked with a yawn.

"I might go over to Mrs. Hamilton's later."

Mom grimaced. "Take her something sweet."

I grinned. "She'll probably feed it to her cat."

The timer went off, and I opened the oven door a crack. So far, no Vesuvius. After putting on a pair of oven mitts, I carefully lifted the soufflé from the rack and set it on the counter. Mom walked over and peered down.

"It's puffy," she said encouragingly.

"That's the crown," I informed her. "The soufflé is supposed to be eaten immediately, before it falls." I'd picked up that piece of information from one of my father's cookbooks. And not only his. I'd been reading cookbooks since I was ten. Famous chefs offer lots of great advice on cooking. And on life too, if you think about it, since their kitchens are their world.

Mom examined my creation. "I'm ready, if you are." She grabbed two clean plates from the dishwasher and I carried my soufflé to the table. I let it rest for a moment between us, thinking how great it would be if Dad could be here to see this. It was his own recipe, after all. And he'd be so pleased to see that I'd pulled it off.

"Not bad," he might say. Or, "Soufflés can be tricky." Which is high praise, coming from the creator of "Carson's Cuisine." Because my father always insists that no recipe is perfect.

The phone rang. Mom frowned. I got up to answer it.

"Hello? Evie? Is that you?"

"Yes, Mrs. Hamilton. Is everything all right?"

"Well, that's just it. I don't know. I can't find Millie. Could you come over and look for her?"

I snuck a peek at the soufflé. Good, still puffy. "We're having breakfast. I'll be over in about twenty minutes."

I could sense her scowl, boring into me through the telephone. Mom was right. That woman did need something sweet.

"She's been gone since last night," Mrs. H said angrily, as if Millie's disappearance were somehow my fault.

"Okay, I'll be right over," I said. "Would you like me to bring some of my soufflé?"

Silence. She had already hung up.

Turning, I caught sight of my mother's expression. Deflated now, sort of like the newly sunken mess on the table in front of her.

"I'm so sorry, honey," she said, eyeing the caved-in soufflé. "Can we still have some?"

I suddenly felt caved in too. Maybe it was better that Dad wasn't here to see this, after all. "Might as well," I replied.

"Mrs. Hamilton's cat doesn't seem to be around to eat any of it."

By the time I got to Mrs. H's house, the temperature outside must have reached ninety-eight degrees. Sweat trickled down the backs of my legs and into my sneakers. Maybe I'd call my friend Karyn later. She lived in an apartment complex with a swimming pool.

As I entered the yard, I surveyed the area for Millie the cat. Not up in the oak tree. Then I inspected the front of the house. No cat on the roof or in the eaves. I listened for cries of distress. Once I'd found Millie caught in the rain gutter, hissing angrily, but she wasn't there today. That crazy cat was meaner than its owner. And older. She was probably on her ninth life already. Oh, well. Maybe Millie had found her way back home since Mrs. H's phone call.

There was no response when I rang the bell, but Mrs. Hamilton was nearly deaf, so I figured she simply hadn't heard. I knocked on the door. Loudly. Still no answer. Carefully, I cracked the door open. It groaned in protest.

"Evie? Is that you?"

Mrs. H was calling from somewhere in the back

of the house. Her voice sounded funny. As if she were talking through a tin can.

"Evie!" she called again, with more volume this time.

I hurried into the back bedroom, where I found Mrs. Hamilton sitting on the floor, breathing heavily.

"Well, what are you staring at? Help me up!" she demanded.

I bent down and grabbed her by the elbows, but I was afraid they'd snap in my hands. I reached for her shoulders, and her ice-cold fingers gripped my arm as I lifted her onto the bed. She was as light as a potato chip. Lighter than her cat. And I was scared.

I sat on the bed next to Mrs. Hamilton and waited for her breathing to slow. "Are you all right?" I asked. Talk about stupid questions.

"Of course I'm all right," she grumbled, smoothing the skirt in her lap with trembling fingers. "I thought I'd look for Millie under the bed. But once I got down there, I couldn't get back up."

"Maybe I should call my mom."

"You'll do no such thing. I'm fine. Fit as a fiddle."

I knew better than to argue with her.

"Did you bring any of that whatever it was you

were making with you?" Mrs. Hamilton asked. The old woman's breathing was back to normal, along with her nasty disposition.

"No," I said apologetically. "I can run back home and get some."

"Never mind," she barked. "Just find my cat."

I had no idea where to start. "When did you see her last?"

"How should I know? My memory's not that good. I fed her last night, though. I remember that." But Mrs. Hamilton didn't sound as if she remembered it at all. She sounded unsure, and frightened.

"Okay," I said reassuringly. "So Millie hasn't been gone *too* long."

I helped Mrs. H stand up and then led her into the kitchen.

"Can I get you anything? Some water, maybe?"

"Just find my cat!" she repeated, and I could see that her rapid blinking was barely holding back tears. How long had that cat *really* been gone, I wondered?

I opened the back door and a gust of hot air stung my face, like steam. The lake's surface rippled in response, and I wondered if the cat had somehow wandered in and drowned.

With one hand shading my eyes, I scanned the yards along the shoreline, then stepped outside.

"Millie!" I yelled. "Millie! Where are you?"

No answer. All I heard was the soft rhythm of water lapping against sand.

Evie's Mount Vesuvius Omelet Soufflé

1 teaspoon water
½ cup finely chopped green onion
½ cup finely chopped green pepper
Dash salt
Dash pepper
Dash cayenne pepper
4 egg yolks
5 egg whites
A few drops lemon juice

🐜 Preheat oven to 400 degrees F.

🐜 Combine the water with the onions and pepper in a medium saucepan over medium-high heat. Cover and cook about 15 minutes. Uncover and cook over high heat for about 5 more minutes. Add salt, pepper, and cayenne to taste. Set aside to cool slightly.

🍃 In a large bowl, beat the egg yolks with an electric mixer until very thick and light in color. In another large bowl, beat the egg whites with the lemon juice until stiff peaks form. Stir the vegetables into the yolks, then add in the whites.

🍃 Lightly coat an 8-inch soufflé dish with vegetable oil and spoon in the soufflé mixture. Bake for about 15 minutes, or until puffy and browned on top. Serves two.

Evie's Kitchen Tip #1
The faster a soufflé rises, the faster it falls.

CHAPTER 2

Portioning

"Cut and chop a lot of onions at one time
and get the misery over with."
—Heloise

When Dad first moved out, I didn't really catch on to the idea that he wasn't going to be around anymore. After a while, it hit me, though. The spaces in the house began to grow, and I became used to a new way of doing things, a new structure in our lives. Now I didn't need to be bothered about Dad barging in on me in the bathroom. I no longer worried about tipping over his half-full *Frugal Gourmet* coffee mug whenever I was clicking away on the computer. And I didn't fret anymore about accidentally sitting on his reading glasses or stacking his precious pots and pans in the wrong order on our kitchen shelves.

But my head still jerked when the front door swung open at night. And I continued to clip recipes and cooking tips, stockpiling them in my old Nike shoe box. That had been Dad's idea—the clippings, not the shoe box. Now, whenever I found a really good recipe, I'd think, "Wait till I show him this one," forgetting that my father would not be in the kitchen that evening, chopping onions and warbling like Pavarotti.

Dad collected recipes too, of course. That was his job. But he filed them in a wooden cabinet, all neatly organized and alphabetized. One day he found four different methods of preparing asparagus, and you would have thought he'd discovered buried treasure in the backyard, the way he raced down the hall to the study. Dad was in such a hurry to file those recipes that he tripped over the dog and ended up spraining his ankle.

But the hall grew empty after he left. And the contents of my father's wooden files were packed in boxes and transported across town in a moving van. All except *one* of those asparagus recipes, which I found behind the couch while I was vacuuming one afternoon. I stared at the list of measurements and ingredients, my eyes welling up. And I think that's when I really knew what it meant to have him *gone*. When you wanted someone to be there so much, it made you almost sick to your stomach.

Mom found me there in the study, propped up against the vacuum cleaner and crying like my heart had been swallowed whole. She didn't have to ask.

"I want him to come back," I wailed.

Mom's features froze. No emotion. It was as if she'd made herself numb in order to get through it all. I think we both had. And I suddenly wanted to hug her and try to make her feel better, or maybe it was only to make *me* feel better. All I know is that the two of us were suddenly wrapped around each other, sobbing together. And I thought, Okay, this is how it's going to be. Just me and Mom. We're going to have to make this be enough.

So we changed our shape, and we made ourselves fit into all those empty corners of the house, filling up the spaces like water in a sponge. And Mom got used to doing things like fixing leaky faucets and lugging the Christmas lights down from the crawl space in the attic. I started taking out the garbage without being asked, and I even washed my mother's car a few times.

But mostly, I cooked.

The kitchen had always been Dad's domain, his retreat. And my mom was happy to leave it to him. Preparing meals was something she did out of necessity, not for enjoyment. Besides, Mom had piano students wandering in and out most afternoons and into the evenings too. Who had time to make dinner?

Sometimes, when I was feeling particularly uncharitable, I couldn't help blaming my mother a little for what had happened. I mean, if she'd merely shown a *little* interest in the food Dad was preparing, he might not have left us. Right? If she'd shooed some of those musical prodigies out of the house after dinner, maybe the three of us could have embarked on moonlight walks around the lake with Mousse or stayed up and played Parcheesi together until bedtime.

Parcheesi? Who was I kidding? Nobody I knew stayed up playing board games with her mom and dad. And the one time I took a moonlight walk with Mousse, he'd dug up a dead raccoon. But still... Mom and Dad had begun to lead separate lives right here. While living in the same house. When did this happen? And why didn't I see it? Could I have done anything about it? Was all of this my fault?

Right after Dad moved out, my aunt Tricia came to stay with us for a week. Big mistake. If I had to hear her call my dad an SOB one more time, I thought I'd hurl one of his saucepans at her. She kept telling Mom to throw out all his leftover stuff—like those big bulky sweaters he handed down to me and his collection of silly aprons that people had given him over the years. Man! Aunt Tricia just didn't get it. That was all we had left of him around here. Why couldn't she let it be?

Of course, it's not as if we never saw Dad anymore. Nothing like that. I went over to his apartment (excuse me, to his and *Angie's* apartment) at least once a week. And he dropped by the house now and then to collect his mail and trim the hedges. He and Mom were always polite when he showed up. Kind of like two strangers who'd bumped into each other in the frozen food aisle of the supermarket.

Another thing that changed was the hallway. We used to have family pictures lining the walls in even rows, like railroad tracks. But after the divorce, Dad took most of these with him. I guess he figured the pictures were *his*, since he'd photographed the majority of them.

So now, all traces of us as a family were gone, all those pictures of Dad and me grinning with the Powwow Princesses or that really big photo of the three of us happily snow skiing in North Carolina. Okay, I never actually made it down that hill, but even so, you can't wipe out all those memories just by hiding photographs of them. Can you?

A mirror hangs in our hallway now. But every time I pass it, no one smiles back at me.

Some other changes were more subtle but just as noticeable. Like the way my dad's name changed. Example: One afternoon I overheard Mom talking on the phone.

"No, I'm sorry, Mrs. Hamilton. Evie can't be there tomorrow. She'll be at her father's for the weekend." *Her father.* Not her dad. Or Dave. Or even David. It was as if his real name was now off-limits or something. And of course, Aunt Tricia simply chose the

SOB alternative, or worse names that I shouldn't repeat.

My dad wasn't an SOB. Not really. That's what made it so hard. He was still my dad. And I loved him. But I was expected to do it from across a lake. My feelings for my father had suddenly turned into a conscious effort, something I was forced to think about and actually do, instead of a piece of me that was sort of *inside*, like it had always been. I couldn't just throw that old part of me away. Could I?

So I cooked. It made me happy. Plus, it was the little piece of him I could keep around.

And Mom taught piano.

And Aunt Tricia finally went back to Michigan.

We were making it work.

Millie had been missing a few days now, so Mrs. Hamilton was more cantankerous than ever. I'd decided not to tell Mom about finding her on the floor the other day, but I wasn't sure why. Maybe I was afraid Mrs. H would have to be put away in some nursing home. I didn't think that would sit too well with a person quite so feisty.

"I've called all the animal shelters in Clermont

Lake," Mrs. H complained to me, "but those people are no help at all."

I didn't want to remind Mrs. Hamilton of the many dangers (most of them with sharp teeth) lurking around the lakeshore at night. If Millie had not returned by now, there had to be a reason, and it probably wasn't a good one.

"I'll come back later this afternoon," I promised. "And I bet Millie will be right here at the front door, yowling her head off."

Mrs. Hamilton pursed her lips. "Bring something to eat when you come."

Dad called the next morning while I was kneading a giant blob of biscuit dough. Like remote radar, he always seemed to know when I was cooking.

"Is your mother home?" he asked. *Your mother.* Mom's name had changed now too.

"She's with a piano student. Wanna listen?" I held up the telephone receiver so my dad could hear the unbearable sounds coming from the study.

Usually he cracked up when I did stuff like that, but not this time. He sounded breathless on the phone, as if he'd just run around the block or something.

"Oh. I guess I can call back later," he said. Then, almost as an afterthought, "You okay, pumpkin seed?" Funny. I was about to ask him the same thing (only leaving out the *pumpkin seed* part).

"Sure. I'm doing fine. I'm thinking of taking a cooking class later this summer. At the rec center."

"Great!" Dad said enthusiastically. "I'm sure you'll learn a lot." Not exactly the reaction I'd been hoping for. Couldn't he have said something like "you already know how to cook," or "you could probably *teach* that class"?

I glanced at the lump of dough resting on the kitchen counter. Maybe, after this six-week cooking class was over, I could prepare a wonderful meal for my dad. All by myself.

There was a long pause before he spoke again. "I was actually calling with some exciting news. Well, I think it's exciting, anyway."

I pounded on the biscuit dough with one fist, waiting for my dad to go on.

"Ummm . . . Angie visited the doctor today, her obstetrician, actually. And when he went to take the baby's heartbeat, he heard an echo. At first Dr. Gordon was kind of worried, but then he ordered an ultrasound—do you know what that is, Evie?"

I took my fist out of the dough, wondering where all this was going. "It's kind of like a picture of what's inside of her, isn't it?"

"That's right. They use sound waves to form the outline of the picture. Anyway, we saw the results of the ultrasound, and you'll never guess. Angie is pregnant with *twins*! In just three more months, you're going to have a brother *and* a sister. How about that?"

I hadn't really thought about Angie's baby being a brother or a sister, to tell you the truth. But now I guess I had to. Something inside me shifted uncomfortably.

"That's terrific, Dad," I lied. What was Mom going to say about this? She'd flip. And Aunt Tricia? That woman would be carrying on for weeks.

"Don't tell your mom, okay?" Dad said quickly. "I want to surprise her."

She was going to be surprised, all right.

"I'll call back later," my father went on. "When will the lessons be over?"

"I'm not sure. You want me to have her call you back instead?"

"Fine, yes. That'll be fine. Have her call me." Dad sounded so excited that I couldn't help being infected by his excitement too. Twins. Wow. Just when you thought things couldn't get any weirder.

"Well, I'd better get back to Angie. I'll talk to you later, pumpkin seed."

"Okay, Dad. Bye."

"I love you, Evie," Dad added, and then he was gone. Taking in my father's news, I considered the soundless phone in my hand. I guess I should have been jealous, or angry. But mainly I felt sort of empty.

Wouldn't you know it? I'd just gotten used to having him gone, and now he was about to start a whole new family. I wasn't sure how I was supposed to react.

But Mom knew exactly how to react. When she talked to Dad after dinner, she sat down at the kitchen table and laughed. She actually laughed! In fact, Mom was still laughing about it as we rinsed the dishes.

"Twins!" she shrieked. "Oh, this is wonderful. Priceless. I couldn't have come up with anything better! Your father is really getting what he deserves now."

I frowned. "But he's thrilled about it, Mom."

She hooted again, but the noises coming out of her mouth sounded odd. Almost fake. "Well, of course he is. He's spreading his genes all over Clermont Lake! It's worse than a rabbit farm!"

I don't know why I felt the need to defend him, but I did. "Come on. Can't you be a *little* bit happy for him, Mom?"

"Oh, I'm happy all right. I'm ecstatic!" Mom shouted. She was so worked up, there were tears streaming down her face. "Think of all those diapers and bottles. At his age! And he'll need two of everything. Two pacifiers. Two strollers. Two car seats. Two cribs. And then later . . . two bicycles. Two sets of braces. And two college tuitions!"

My mother was crying big time now. But I don't

think it had anything to do with laughter. Tears trickled down both of her cheeks, along with sticky streaks of blackish-blue mascara. And her nose was running too.

I reached down into the soapy water and held her hand, not sure what else to do. I guess maybe Mom felt as left out as I did.

We stood there in front of the sink for a long while. The water got cold, and I fetched a dish towel and handed it to her. She dried her hands and then dabbed at her eyes, finally giving a tiny shrug.

"I'm being mean and spiteful, Evie. Do you think I'm awful?"

"No," I answered truthfully. "You can't help it."

Her shoulders stiffened, and I knew she wasn't quite sure how to take that.

I hurriedly went on. "What I mean is, I feel that way too. And I can't help it either."

Mom nodded. Then she turned the hot water on and began refilling the sink. I continued rinsing.

"Hey," I said. "Want to hear something *really* mean and spiteful?"

She studied me, mascara still smudged across her face.

"I believe Dad actually has *three* college tuitions to worry about, not just two."

This time, Mom's laughter was loud—and very real.

Evie's Epicurean Biscuits

2 cups all-purpose flour
½ teaspoon salt
1 tablespoon baking powder
1 tablespoon sugar
6 tablespoons cold butter
¾ cup milk
¾ cup feta cheese, rinsed and crumbled
1 egg yolk, mixed with 1 tablespoon water

Preheat the oven to 425 degrees F. Sift the dry ingredients into a large mixing bowl. Quickly cut the butter into the mixture with a pastry blender, until it resembles coarse oatmeal. Pour in the milk, add the cheese, and stir by hand for about 30 seconds to make a soft dough.

🐾 Knead the dough quickly for another 30 seconds on a lightly floured surface. Press the dough flat and fold in half. Repeat pressing down and folding 6 to 8 times. Roll out with a rolling pin to about ½-inch thickness.

🐾 Cut the dough into 1- or 2-inch rounds with a cookie or biscuit cutter. Place on an ungreased baking sheet and brush with the egg-water glaze. Bake for 12 to 15 minutes. Makes about one dozen biscuits.

Evie's Kitchen Tip #2

Instead of using a cookie or biscuit cutter, you can drop dough by the spoonful onto a baking sheet. These are called "cat-head" biscuits.

CHAPTER 3

Accommodation

"Do not crowd the pan."
—Tom Colicchio

Before I go any further, I should probably tell you what it's like when I visit Dad and Angie. They're both nice to me and all, maybe a little too nice. And I get lots of time to play with Mousse, which is great. It's just that I don't really feel comfortable there. The furniture is all brand-new, and the kitchen floor is spotless. There's not a single food stain on their white leather sofa, so I'm afraid to eat anything in front of the TV. And I'm extra careful to wipe the soles of my shoes before setting foot on the new carpet.

Not that Dad or Angie has ever asked me to wipe my feet—or keep food out of the living room. But I am uneasy about it anyway, imagining that the minute I leave, Angie is going to whisk through the entire place with a broom and a dustpan.

I guess what I'm trying to say is that I don't have any sense of belonging there. I mean, at home Mom sometimes gripes at me to help her with the dishes or pick up after myself. Other times, she just lets me go off to my room and listen to CDs, or talk on the phone with my friends. There are entire evenings when we don't share a single word until it's time to say "good night." And we're both okay with that.

But Angie is about as different from Mom as you can get. She wears power suits and Nikes instead of sweatshirts or blue jeans. And for her, silence is definitely *not* golden. Angie always seems determined to have some sort of "conversation" with me. She read somewhere that stepmoms should spend time alone with their new stepchildren—a sort of "quality" time, set aside to share ideas and opinions.

"I think the billboards along Mason Avenue are disgraceful, don't you?" Angie said to me one evening. "Those signs block the entire view of Clermont

Lake, and they're a safety hazard besides. A driver could be reading one of them and steer his car right off the road! What do you think, Evie?"

She paused, and I realized that I was supposed to respond.

"Uh-huh." My father had run an errand and left me here with his twenty-five-year-old wife. There should be laws against this kind of thing!

"Of course, Dave thinks I'm crazy, carrying on about those billboards. Some of the ads are for our own newspaper, wouldn't you know? Still, this town is in need of some long-range growth planning, don't you think? There's too much development. Before you know it, all the trees will be gone and the only thing we'll have left are strip malls and car dealerships."

Mousse let out a little whimper. He was squatting near the front door, massive tail wagging, and I knew he was itching to get out of here. That made two of us.

"Well," I said brightly, "looks like Mousse could use a walk."

As soon as Mousse heard the word *walk,* his ears stood up like two small flags in a strong wind. I grabbed his leash from the kitchen counter and hooked it to his collar, reaching for the doorknob.

"Have fun," Angie said, flashing me with all her teeth. She was nice, but sometimes I wished she would stop trying so hard.

Once again, it was hotter than fried eggs outside. I kicked off my sandals and led Mousse down to the water's edge so he could frolic in the mud. I'd have to make sure I hosed him off completely before letting him back in the condo. Mom's rule, not Dad's. She didn't want Angie to think I was totally devoid of manners.

Secretly, I wondered what Angie would do if I let Mousse drip fat blobs of smelly brown ooze all over her new carpet. Would she yell at me? I actually hoped she would. Then at least I'd know she was human.

"Evie!" I turned at the sound of my dad's voice. He was running down the grassy slope toward the two of us. "How's my girl?"

"Good," I said, giving him a quick hug. Mousse jumped all over my father's legs, smearing mud on his jeans. Dad stroked the dog's head appreciatively, then began walking along the shore with the two of

us. It reminded me of old times, and I couldn't help glancing across the lake at the row of tiny houses on the opposite shore. I could barely make out the yellow square of light that was Mom's study. She was probably sitting with some kid at the piano right now, tapping out a rhythm with her pencil.

"Did you have a nice talk with Angie?" Dad asked in an offhanded way—a little too offhanded, if you ask me. And it dawned on me—smack!—that my father had left the two of us alone in that condominium on purpose.

"Dad," I answered truthfully, "I don't actually talk with Angie. Mostly, I, umm, listen."

He stopped and whipped around to confront me. I could see that he was angry. "Why can't you just *like* her?" he said. "She is trying so hard to be your friend."

"I don't *dislike* her, Dad," I said. "Jeez. I don't even know her."

He kept staring at me. Maybe he thought that if he did this long enough, I would somehow miraculously change my mind about Angie. Well. I wasn't going to let my father bully me, no matter how much I wanted to make him happy.

"I have plenty of friends, Dad."

The sun was going down behind us, and my father's face was one dark shadow with a glowering gash across it. "Fair enough," he said. "But when you decide you do need another friend, she's here. Okay?"

"Okay," I said, sorry now that I'd disappointed him. But I wasn't in the market for a buddy, and I sure didn't need a second mother, either. Two families and two homes were more than I could handle at the moment, and I felt as if I were being crammed into a space where I hardly had room to breathe.

I remembered a food preparation tip I'd read in a cookbook once: *Do not crowd the pan.*

Exactly.

And now that Angie was preparing for twins, my family was no longer a crowd. It was a horde! The pan was overflowing, its sticky contents slopping over the sides and right into the fire.

Well, maybe I was being too dramatic, but sometimes I did fantasize about sailing away to a private island. Actually, I wished that I could simply travel back in time—to a moment when life was only me and Mom and Dad. Oh, and Mousse. But what time would I choose? A year ago? No, Dad was already on his way out by then. Two years ago? Definitely not! That was the year I got braces. Three years? Yikes! The year of Ms. Timplehauser, the long-term substitute who smelled like mothballs.

Okay. Perhaps going back in time was not the answer. But let's face it. The here and now wasn't looking so great either.

I'd made a red velvet cake earlier that morning, and as soon as I got home, I took it over to Mrs. Hamilton. Millie had been missing for a number of days now, and I was fairly certain that she would not be there this afternoon either.

I was right.

"It's crooked," the woman snapped, squinting at my perfectly proportioned cake. I tried my best to remember that she was merely worried about Millie. That cat was the only thing she had, after all.

"I'm still learning," I said.

Surprisingly, Mrs. Hamilton's face lost some of its edginess. "Aren't we all?" she said softly.

We were quiet for a moment, me thinking about my expanding family and Mrs. H contemplating her shrinking one.

"I got that stupid cat right after Gus passed away," she said. The old woman was staring out the window and across the lake.

"Gus?"

"My husband. You never knew him. Or, well, maybe you did. I think you were just a baby. I remember your mother and father passing by here every day, with you tucked inside one of those little pouch things. You'd be all snuggled up in a little ball, just sleeping away...." Her voice trailed off, and I saw that she had succeeded in doing what I had failed to do earlier. She'd gone back in time.

"So Millie must be thirteen years old too?"

Mrs. H turned to stare at me, her moist eyes trying to take in an older version of the baby she'd been remembering. Then they seemed to clear, and she glanced away again.

"Millie's not coming back, Evie."

Evie's Scrumptious Red Velvet Cake

CAKE:
½ cup shortening
1½ cups sugar
2 eggs
2 ounces red food coloring
2 heaping tablespoons cocoa
1 cup buttermilk
2¼ cups sifted cake flour
1 teaspoon salt
1 teaspoon vanilla
1 teaspoon baking soda
1 tablespoon vinegar

FROSTING:
3 tablespoons flour
1 cup milk
1 cup sugar
1 cup (2 sticks) butter
1 teaspoon vanilla

🍓 Preheat oven to 350 degrees F. Grease and flour two 8-inch cake pans.

🍓 Mix shortening, sugar, and eggs with electric mixer. Make paste out of food coloring and cocoa. By hand, add cocoa mixture to egg mixture. Add buttermilk alternately with flour and salt. Add vanilla. Mix baking soda with vinegar, then add the bubbling mixture to the batter, blending instead of beating.

🍓 Divide batter between prepared cake pans. Bake 25 to 30 minutes, then cool on rack to room temperature before frosting.

🍓 FROSTING: On stovetop, cook flour and milk over low heat until thick, stirring constantly. Cool. Mix sugar, butter, and vanilla until fluffy. Blend milk and flour mixture into sugar mixture. Spread on bottom layer. Place second layer on top, and frost entire cake, using a butter knife dipped in warm water. Makes one 8-inch, 2-layer cake to serve about 10.

Evie's Kitchen Tip #3
To test a cake's doneness, poke it with a piece of raw spaghetti. If it comes out dry, the cake is done!

CHAPTER 4

Coordination

"Organize! Prioritize!"
—Bobby Flay

Dad came over later and took me out to dinner. Just him and me. We did that a lot when he was married to Mom, eating out together so that the two of us could complain about the food and make our own suggestions for improving the menu. We called these outings our *snob dinners*, and Mom wanted nothing to do with them. For her, dinner was dinner. But for us, the meals were an adventure. And we attacked each new menu with gusto and well-trained tastebuds.

"Too much salt," I pronounced, chewing on a mouthful of pork chop.

"And garlic," Dad agreed. "Could use a little more basil, though."

We chewed quietly for a while, both of us remembering our argument by the lake. When my father was finished, he set down his fork.

"I love you, pumpkin seed," he said, out of the blue.

I had just bit into a huge piece of meat and was unable to respond.

"The important stuff will never change between us," he went on. "You know that, don't you?"

"Yeah, sure, Dad," I finally managed to croak.

He sighed. "I wish you'd stop acting like this."

"Like what? I'm not acting like anything."

"You're acting like you don't believe me. And I'm trying to *tell* you. Nothing is ever going to come between you and me. Not Angie. Not the babies. Not even my favorite set of wooden spoons!"

I laughed, and he reached over and tousled my hair.

"If I could have you live with me, you know I would. But your mother and I discussed that.

Besides, you didn't want to change schools. Remember?"

I remembered. "So you took all of our pictures instead."

Dad looked puzzled. "Pictures?"

"Never mind," I said quickly, not wanting to start another argument with him when our meal was going so well. "Can we still have our snob dinners together?"

"Always. Once a month, at least. I promise. And you can choose the restaurant in July. Deal?"

I couldn't help but smile a little. "Deal."

We hugged. And I have to admit that it felt kind of nice.

Monday. Day number one of my cooking class, and I thought I'd be the first up. But when I walked into the kitchen, Mom was already there, with the newspaper spread out in front of her like a fan. She pointed to a small paragraph, and I read over her shoulder: *Missing: Millie, orange-and-black cat with one black ear. Please contact Janine Hamilton, 273 Lakeshore Drive, 555-7738.*

"Who put that in there?" I asked.

"Mrs. Hamilton, probably. You can place classified ads over the phone."

Hmmm. *Janine.* All this time and I'd never bothered to ask Mrs. Hamilton her first name. Janine and Gus. Two people who had lived next door to us since I was an infant. And I'd only now discovered their names.

Mom grabbed a pair of scissors from a drawer and began snipping around Mrs. Hamilton's advertisement.

"Could you pin this up at the rec center when you go in for your cooking class later?"

"Sure." I folded the clipping and put it in my pocket. The phone rang, and I sensed Mom's gaze following me as I picked up the receiver.

"Hello? Yeah, just a minute. She's right here." I mouthed three silent words to my mother as I handed her the phone. "It's a man!"

Mom primped her hair and stood up. "I'll take it in the study," she said hurriedly, before dashing out of the kitchen. What was this all about? I wondered. But I was afraid I already knew.

I could hear Mom talking, but I couldn't quite make out the words. She sounded pretty cheerful, though. Every once in a while, a cackle would erupt from behind the closed door. Weird.

Glancing around the kitchen, I saw no evidence that my mother had attempted to prepare breakfast. So I got started. I swung open the refrigerator door and peered inside. Two containers of peach yogurt, a half-empty carton of milk, orange juice, mushrooms, six eggs, two green onions, and some Swiss cheese. Well. I'd have to make do. Maybe a couple of Swiss mushroom omelets and an orange/peach smoothie from the blender.

I dug around in the cupboards for Dad's old omelet pan and a spatula. Then I grated some cheese. Eventually, Mom came into the kitchen, still bare-foot. She stood next to me, watching me whip up the eggs in a bowl.

"Okay," I finally said. "Who was that?"

Mom started slicing the mushrooms for me. "His name is Brent."

Brent. No last name. This was not good. "And?"

She stopped slicing. "And what?"

"How do you know this guy Brent?"

"You sound like Aunt Tricia!" Mom said with a snort. But I noticed she hadn't answered my question.

"I suppose he was calling you from Mars," I prompted, but my mother simply smirked.

"He's the father of a piano student," she informed me.

"Uh-huh." I decided to let it rest. Mom would fill me in when she was good and ready.

The two of us sat at the table, munching and drinking, and I started to think about my cooking class. Even though I was an experienced cook, I was still nervous about it, never having cooked for anyone but my family or Mrs. Hamilton. I glanced at the wall clock. Class began in two hours, and I still needed to take a shower and wash my hair. But, wait! I'd be a sweaty mess if I walked all the way to the rec center in this heat. Maybe Mom could give me a ride.

"Hey, Mom—" I began.

"Would you stop pestering me about Brent!" Mom said, slamming her cup down on the table between us. I gaped at her.

"I was only going to ask for a ride to the rec center," I said. "My cooking class. Remember?"

Mom seemed bewildered, but then she began to chuckle. "I'm too old for this," she said. Reaching for my hand across the table, she added, "Sorry, Evie."

"Mom, what's going *on?*"

My mother sighed, running her long piano-playing fingers through a tangle of hair. "Brent has invited me to the movies this weekend. And I think I'd like to go."

"Oh." I'd thought as much.

"Is it okay with you?"

Was it? I didn't know. But it wasn't fair to make my mother feel guilty about seeing a movie, if going out with this Brent guy was what she really wanted to do.

"Sure," I said. "Can Karyn come over while you're gone?"

"I don't see why not." Mom appeared relieved, and I was instantly proud of the way I'd handled myself. I mean, what business was it of mine if she wanted to go out on a date with some man I'd never met or seen or even *heard* of before?

My mother began clearing the table. "Why don't you get cleaned up while I do the dishes?" she suggested.

As I left the room, I could hear her humming a little tune to herself. Something by Haydn or Chopin. Mom was really *way* too cheerful this morning.

After getting dropped off at the rec center, I wandered around, searching for the cooking room. A couple of kids were milling about on the basketball courts, so I stopped and asked for directions.

"Cooking?" one boy repeated, as if he'd never heard the word before. He bounced his basketball a few times and passed it off to his friend.

"What you gonna cook?" the other boy asked.

"I don't know," I answered truthfully, and the two of them exploded with laughter. I had no idea what was so funny.

"It's this way," said a voice from behind me, and I swiveled around, expecting to encounter another basketball comedian.

A kid with reddish-brown hair and a mass of freckles stood glaring at me, as if I'd broken some elementary rule of rec-center etiquette. Without another word, he turned and led me into a brick building with two heavy yellow doors.

Once inside, I followed him down a hallway to another set of yellow doors. I certainly hoped he knew where he was taking me. But when we stepped through the double doors, I saw all I needed to see.

At last! The cooking center. This room was enormous! And the place was jam-packed with kitchen equipment and utensils. Six cooking stations lined the walls, each with a sink, sideboard, stove, oven, and a tiny refrigerator. Most of the cubicles were already occupied by students, who were inspecting cupboards and pulling out drawers. On the counter of each station rested an unopened carton of eggs. Oh, no. I certainly hoped we weren't going to tackle a soufflé on our very first morning!

A woman with spiky gray tendrils of hair approached the two of us. She wore a flowery blue dress that swirled about her ankles as she walked, and her leather sandals made a soft padding sound on the white linoleum tiles.

"Corey," she breathed. "How nice to see you again. And who is this?" She and Corey both observed me expectantly.

"Uh . . . Evie . . . Carson."

"So good to have you," the woman said. "I'm Shanti Venu, your cooking master. Why don't you and Corey partner up at station six?"

Corey's freckles reddened, as if this was the last thing he wanted to do. But the two of us crossed the room to the single unoccupied cooking area, and my new partner immediately pulled out a drawer, rooting around for something very important.

"So, you've taken this class before?" I asked. He merely grunted, but I took this sound as a yes.

"Now, class," Shanti said from the center of the cavernous room, "today we are going to learn something which many of you may *think* you already know how to do but which most people do incorrectly. Today we are going to boil an egg."

I rolled my eyes in Corey's direction, but his attention was riveted on Shanti. The cooking master continued. "Boiling eggs is all about timing, not method. Shall we begin?"

This must have been her signal, because all the students began rummaging through their stations for saucepans and spoons. Corey already had his pan under the faucet and was filling it up with water.

"First," Shanti instructed us, "you must cover the eggs with *cold* water. And, ideally, the eggs you start with should be at room temperature, not chilled."

I piled six room-temperature eggs into my saucepan and poured cold water over them. Then I waited for the water to boil. So far, so good.

Shanti walked around the room, checking on our pans of water. "Now, this is where so many people falter in the preparation of boiled eggs," she said earnestly. "Once the water has come to a boil, you must *reduce* the heat and let the water simmer."

We all reduced the heat under our eggs. Unfortunately, one of mine had already cracked. Wispy strings of egg white were bobbing around in the bubbling water, floating like miniature clouds.

"Turn it down a little bit more," Corey said disgustedly.

Shanti glided over to us, like a leaf skimming the surface of a lake. She stared into my pan, her mouth slightly puckered. "That is why you each started with six," she said encouragingly.

The cooking master now held up three fingers in front of the class. "For soft-cooked eggs, remove them three minutes after you have reduced the heat."

Drat! I had no idea how long it had been since I'd reduced the heat. But Corey did. He was removing one of his eggs with a slotted spoon, so I quickly sorted through my collection of spoons and fished one of my eggs out too.

Up went another one of Shanti's fingers. "Allow four minutes for medium-soft-cooked eggs." Medium-soft? What in the heck was that? I decided to leave the rest of mine in until they were good and hard.

"For hard-cooked eggs," Shanti went on, "you should remove the eggs after fifteen minutes. *But—* and here is where so many people fail—you must immediately plunge the eggs into cold water so that the yolks do not become discolored. The perfect egg yolk should be yellow, not tinged with green or brown."

I foraged in desperation for another pan to fill with cold water. How many pans were we going to need just to boil a few eggs?

"Here." Corey shoved a saucepan at me and began pouring tap water into another. Jeez! He didn't have to be so snotty about it. How did I know eggs had to be plunged?

As I pivoted to take the pan from him, the hem of my sleeve snagged itself on the long wooden handle.

Crash! The saucepan hit the floor and then bounced, cold water splashing onto the tiles and all over Corey's spotless Reeboks. I didn't offer an apology. What could I say to him, anyway? Humiliated, I sopped up the spilled water with a dishtowel and began to refill the pan myself.

At last, our task was finished. I had never concentrated so hard in my life. Who would have thought that boiling an egg could be so complicated? Or so exhausting?

As Shanti drifted past each station, her students sliced their eggs in half for her, and she examined the results. Thank goodness, my four remaining egg yolks were all as round and yellow as the sun. The cooking master's face lit up, and she patted my hand.

"Nicely done, Evie," she said, her words wafting over me like puffs of wind. "Your father would be proud."

She twirled off to another station, and Corey leaned his head toward mine.

"Your father?" he asked.

"David Carson," I answered with a grin. "You know, 'Carson's Cuisine'?" Now maybe this arrogant partner of mine would be a little more impressed. Or a bit nicer to me, at least.

"You've got to be kidding," he said with a sneer.

By one o'clock I was starving. As it turned out, we were not allowed to eat our boiled eggs because Shanti was going to demonstrate deviled eggs next week. All of us were instructed to wrap up the eggs and leave them in our classroom refrigerators.

As I walked home, the afternoon sun shone across the lake's surface, reflecting the long-limbed cypress trees lining its shore. The dark water was as still as ice. But the calm, silent air above it was so hot and suffocating, I seriously contemplated jumping into the lake with all my clothes on. In fact, as soon as I got home, I intended to rush straight to my room and change into a swimsuit.

Mom was seated at the kitchen table when I walked through the back door. She regarded me numbly, her eyes wet.

"Evie," she said, "Mrs. Hamilton called. They've found Millie."

Evie's Savory Swiss Mushroom Omelet

OMELET:
2 or 3 eggs
¼ teaspoon salt
Dash pepper
Nonstick cooking spray
1 teaspoon butter

FILLING:
1 tablespoon vegetable oil
6-8 ounces white mushrooms, sliced
1 medium onion, finely chopped
½ cup shredded Swiss cheese

Whisk eggs in a bowl with salt and pepper. Spray omelet pan or small skillet with nonstick spray. Add butter and heat over high heat until butter is foaming but not browned. Pour in eggs; keep pulling edges up with fork or spatula, until all liquid is set. (If you like the interior of your omelet well-cooked, you can flip the eggs before adding filling.)

FILLING:

🦐 Heat oil in heavy skillet over medium heat. Sauté mushrooms and onion until golden brown, stirring constantly, until tender. Sprinkle mixture on top of the cooked omelet; add shredded cheese. Fold and roll out onto serving dish. Serves two.

Evie's Kitchen Tip #4

To test to see if an egg is fresh, immerse it in a pan of cool, salted water. If it sinks, it's fresh. If it floats, throw it away!

CHAPTER 5

Cultivation

"Food is about nurturing."
—Ina Garten, the Barefoot Contessa

They turned out to be a couple of early-morning joggers who had discovered Millie by the side of the road a few blocks away from our house. Millie seemed to have been struck by a car, and the two women hadn't known how to get in touch with the owner until they'd seen Mrs. Hamilton's description of Millie in the newspaper. The joggers called as soon as they read the advertisement.

Mrs. H did not take the news well. She immediately phoned our house, in the hopes that my mom and I would go and retrieve Millie's body. Mom said she'd talk to me the minute I got home.

I could actually picture Mrs. H, after she heard the truth about her cat's disappearance. I saw the old woman turning white, crumpling to the floor like a dropped shirt.

"Why did those people have to call her at all?" I said angrily. "Mrs. Hamilton would be a lot happier believing that a couple of kids found her cat and took it home with them."

Mom let out a long breath. "You know that's not true, Evie. Besides, she had a pretty good idea something like this had happened anyway. Isn't it better that she knows now for sure?"

I didn't think so.

"Let me grab a box and some towels from the garage."

We drove slowly around the block, searching for the intersection Mrs. H had described to my mother. Dread hovered over me like black smoke.

"Maybe someone already picked the cat up," I said hopefully, as Mom's car came to an abrupt stop. Through the window I spied an orange-and-black shape near the side of the road. The body was partially covered with oak leaves, and I suddenly had an awful thought. What if some carnivorous creature had found Millie and dragged her remains over there?

Mom took my hand, and we stepped carefully across the pavement to where the cat lay motionless. My mother stretched a towel out on the ground, and I draped another one over Millie's body before lifting her onto the frayed terry cloth, which smelled faintly of gasoline. Perhaps we should have given Mrs. Hamilton's pet something more dignified to lie on, I thought, and I started to cry.

"Do you want to go back to the car for a while?" Mom asked.

"No. I'm okay."

Millie was surprisingly light, and I realized that I had never picked her up before. In life, that cat was too feisty to let anyone get ahold of her for long. She was an independent animal, as Mrs. Hamilton always liked to say.

Mom opened the cardboard box, and I lowered Millie inside. Then we carried the box to the car and drove home. It took forever. The world outside my mother's Chevy passed by, but I was blind to all of it, completely drained.

Mrs. H was sitting in her rocking chair by the front window, waiting for us. She'd probably been in that same spot for hours. I carried the box inside and set it on the floor in front of her. She didn't even glance down at Millie's cardboard coffin, but who could blame her? I placed a hand on her bony shoulder.

"Mrs. Hamilton? Millie looked ... pretty okay. I mean, she seemed all right, you know? Kind of peaceful."

The old woman finally peered down at the box by her feet and then back at me. "Will you help me bury her?" she asked.

My stomach lurched. Finding Millie's body and wrapping it up had been hard enough. All of this was just too much. I shot a peek at my mom, who was giving me her don't-you-dare-say-no look.

"Sure," I managed.

The three of us walked out to a corner of Mrs. Hamilton's yard, where she had already propped a shovel against the side of the house.

"I thought maybe she'd like to rest under this oak tree," Mrs. H said, with a touch of her old crankiness. "Considering we could never get her *out* of it."

So we buried Millie in the shade of her favorite hiding spot. And Mrs. Hamilton placed a small rock headstone over the rounded mound of dirt.

As Mom and I trudged back to our house, I shoved both fists into the pockets of my jeans, and something crinkled beneath the fingers of my right hand.

It was the ad Mrs. H had placed in the newspaper only this morning. I hadn't remembered to pin the clipping up at the rec center. It didn't really matter now.

"Do you suppose she'll ever get another cat?" I asked.

Mom opened the back door and stepped into the kitchen. "Maybe, but not right away. She needs time to adjust, don't you think?"

I remembered how Mom and I had been, right after Dad left—the hollow spaces in the house and the way we'd tended to skirt around them for a while, avoiding all that emptiness. As much as I hated to admit it, Aunt Tricia had done us a favor by shoving us into those corners. She'd gotten us moving again.

Mrs. Hamilton might spend the rest of her life sitting in her rocking chair if she didn't find a reason to get moving too. Chasing after that cat had given her something to grouse and complain about. Let's face it. Millie was her only reason to continue puttering around every day. Well. Mrs. Hamilton definitely needed some shoving now, I decided. But how would I shove her? And *where*?

"So, will you be all right on Saturday?" Mom was asking, interrupting my thoughts.

"Saturday?"

"Yes." Mom's cheeks and neck turned pink as she tugged at the collar of her blouse. "I'm going to the movies with Brent. Did you forget?"

To tell you the truth, I *had* forgotten. Mom's timing was really rotten sometimes.

"I'll be okay," I said. "Karyn's coming over. And we're making pizza from scratch."

Mom's mouth stretched into a fake grin. "Sounds like fun!"

Then stay and make pizza with us, I wanted to say. But I didn't.

I went off to my room, abandoning the idea of a swim in the lake. My head felt so heavy right now, I'd probably sink straight to the bottom anyway. The phone rang and I grabbed it before Mom answered in the kitchen.

It was Dad. "Hi there, pumpkin seed. How is everything?"

"Rotten," I said. "Mrs. Hamilton's cat got hit by a car."

"Oh. Does Mrs. Hamilton need anything?"

"No," I answered dully. "Mom and I went and got

the cat out of the street. Then we helped Mrs. H bury it in her backyard."

There was a long silence. "I'm sorry, honey. Is there something I can do?"

You could give Mousse back to me. "No. Mom says Mrs. Hamilton needs time to adjust to Millie being gone."

"Speaking of your mother, is she home?"

"Yeah. She's got a big date this weekend."

There was a substantially longer silence. "A date? Is it with anyone I know?"

"His name is Brent. His kid takes piano lessons with her."

Dad let out a phony little chuckle. I could tell my father was dying to grill me further, but he resisted. "Well, I'm sure he's a great guy. But if your mother has a moment, I need to talk to her about borrowing the lawn mower."

I set the phone down and left to find Mom, wondering how people could plan dates and borrow lawn mowers when someone's cat had just died.

Back in my room, I flopped onto the bed. My T-shirt was damp with sweat after digging the shallow grave, and I was too exhausted to change out of my smelly clothes. I considered what Mrs. Hamilton might be doing right now. Sitting in her rocker? Tossing out Millie's bowls and brushes and cat vitamins? Then again, maybe Mrs. H wasn't doing anything at all. Maybe she was lying on her bed, like me. Trying not to think about lost pets.

Evie's Heavenly Homemade Pizza

¼ cup warm water
1 package active dry yeast
3¼ cups all-purpose flour
1 teaspoon salt, plus more to taste
1 teaspoon oil
1 (6-ounce) can tomato paste, diluted with
   6 ounces water
¾ cup mozzarella cheese, grated
Dash oregano
Dash basil
1 cup grated Parmesan cheese
1 tablespoon olive oil

🐾 In a bowl, dissolve the yeast in the warm water, mixing well. Set the yeast aside for 10 minutes. Sift the flour and salt into a large bowl. Gradually work the yeast mixture into the flour. Flour your hands and use your knuckles and fists to work the dough until it is smooth and elastic. Form the dough into a ball and wrap it loosely in a clean cotton cloth. Leave it in the bowl in a warm, sheltered place to rise, or cover the bowl with a cloth, for at least 30 minutes. Preheat oven to 450 degrees F.

🍞 Oil a rectangular or circular pizza pan and use your fingertips to gently stretch out the dough to cover the bottom. Spread diluted tomato paste over the dough. Spread the grated mozzarella cheese on top of the tomato. Sprinkle with the salt, basil, oregano, and Parmesan cheese. Drizzle with the olive oil and bake in the oven for about 20 minutes. Serves four.

Evie's Kitchen Tip #5
If you eat uncooked dry yeast, it will continue to grow inside your intestines. Eeew!

CHAPTER 6

Manipulation

*"The most important things to
a chef are his tools."*
—Tyler Florence

The front doorbell rang. Boyfriend Brent. I stayed right where I was, stretched out on the bed with a pillow jammed over my head. I wasn't going to be mannerly and say hello, the way I knew Mom wanted me to.

Knock, knock. "Evie?"

My bedroom door opened a crack and Mom poked her head in. She had her purple eyelids on this evening.

"I'm leaving now, honey. And I hope you and

Karyn enjoy yourselves. We can have a good long talk tomorrow."

I lifted a corner of the pillow. "Okay."

"Maybe I'll even get up early and we can have breakfast together."

"As long as it's not boiled eggs," I mumbled.

"Pardon?"

"Nothing. Never mind. Breakfast sounds fine."

"Have fun tonight."

And she was gone. I could smell the gardenia perfume that Mom wore for special occasions. Then it was gone too. The front door slammed, and a car motor started noisily. Wheels scrunched on the gravel driveway. Quickly, I ran to the window to check out Brent's car. A Lexus, wouldn't you know.

"So what does this Brent person look like?" Karyn asked me later.

We were smothering my homemade pizza dough with tomato paste and grating mozzarella cheese.

"I didn't actually see him."

"No way! Your mom goes on her first date, and you don't even check the guy out?"

"This isn't her first date. Mom went out on plenty of dates before she met Dad."

Karyn stopped grating and studied me. I knew what was coming. Karyn was always watching shows like *Oprah* and *Dr. Phil.* Personally, I preferred reading to watching TV.

"You analyze everything, Evie. Can't you stop thinking for once?"

"I don't want to talk about this now, okay?" I said.

"Okay," Karyn said. But I knew it wasn't.

"Listen, it's not like I think Mom and Dad are going to get back together. I just don't think my mother is . . . ready."

Karyn said nothing, which said plenty.

"All right, all right. It's me who's not ready. Is that what you want to hear?"

"Oprah only wants to hear the truth, Evie," she said, holding out her spoon as if it were a microphone.

I threw a spatula at her. "Then maybe she'd like to hear the truth about my obnoxious cooking partner at the rec center."

I described Corey in detail, along with Shanti and her flowing skirt. And my broken egg. And the spilled water. And the drenched Reeboks. After a while, the entire fiasco sounded funny, even to me. Talking the whole thing out offered me some perspective. And it struck me then that I'd missed a number of chances to discuss this week's catastrophes with my mother.

Had Mom wanted to confide in me too? About Brent? Was she nervous, going out with someone after all these years? Was she excited? Terrified? I'd never taken the time to ask her.

Back when Dad first left, Mom and I talked and hung around together a lot, and it turned out to be sort of fun. We rented sappy videos, attempted to cook (without any of Dad's cookbooks around), and ended up eating mass quantities of takeout food. But the two of us hadn't sobbed our way through a sad movie in a long time.

"Maybe you should show Corey what you can really do on Monday," Karyn suggested.

Yeah. I could still see Corey smirking at me after my egg exploded in that pan of bubbling water. What I needed was to prove to him that I could really cook. And I knew exactly *how* to do it. With my one single irresistible recipe.

"Hey," I said to Karyn, "before you go home, wanna help me bake some chocolate chip cookies with pecans and coconut?"

In the middle of the night there was a knock on my bedroom door.

"Come in," I said groggily, not bothering to lift my head from the pillow.

I could tell immediately that something was wrong. Mom's eyes appeared to be swollen, and her purple eyeshadow was all smeary.

"How'd your evening with Karyn go?" Mom sat down directly on top of my right foot. "Ooops. Sorry," she said.

"Tonight went okay," I replied, rescuing my foot. "We made pizza and chocolate chip cookies. A real junk food jamboree."

Mom wrinkled her nose. Then she grabbed a Kleenex and blew into it. "Is that why you're not sleeping? All that rich food?"

I wasn't sleeping because she'd woken me up! "I guess so," I said to be nice.

"Did you watch any good movies?"

Uh-oh. Mom was in the mood to talk, and I was

too tired to even move my lips. I propped myself up to take a peek at the clock on my nightstand.

"It's three in the morning," Mom said. No wonder her eyes were red. It was already Sunday!

"Did you just get home?" I asked, suddenly wide awake.

Mom smiled ruefully. "No, I've been home for a while. Listen, Evie, I know you're not real wild about me seeing Brent." She was right. "But you wouldn't be wild about anyone I went out with now, isn't that true?"

I pulled my blankets up under my chin. "Probably," I admitted.

Mom looked away from me and then down at her hands, to the spot on her finger where a wedding band used to be. Her voice sounded hoarse. "Sometimes—even now—I wake up in the middle of the night and I forget that Dad doesn't live with us anymore. Then I try to go back to sleep so that I can keep on forgetting it." She shrugged. "It never works."

"But Mom, if you feel that way, then—oh, never mind."

"What? What were you going to say, Evie?"

I was stepping in some real sticky stuff here. "Forget it."

Mom gave my leg a shake through the blankets. "No, talk to me. What's bothering you?"

"Well, I know it's been more than a year and everything...but if you still miss Dad, then *why* would you want to go out with somebody else?"

Mom blew her nose again. "That's exactly why, honey."

I sat up, hugging my pillow. "But everything would be so different, wouldn't it? I mean, what if the new guy doesn't laugh at any of your jokes? Or suppose he talks with his mouth full, or he can't even *cook*?"

"I didn't go out with Brent so that I could pretend he was your father, Evie. In fact, I didn't go out with *anyone* for over a year. That's a pretty long time to be lonely, don't you think? So I said to myself, Well, are you going to keep sitting around waiting for Mr. Perfect to come along? Or are you going to take a chance and go out with a guy and maybe have a terrible time or maybe have an okay time? And I gave it a try."

"And what happened?"

Mom fidgeted with her necklace. "I had a terrible time. Brent talked about his Lexus all night."

As much as I didn't enjoy the idea of my mother dating anyone, I still didn't want her to have a terrible time doing it. "I never knew that you were lonely," I mumbled.

"Only at three o'clock in the morning," she said, giving my leg another squeeze.

"And I'm sorry I didn't come out to say hello to Brent," I added.

"I know."

"Can I ask you something else?"

She regarded me warily, bracing herself.

"If you're so lonely, do you think maybe we could ask Dad to give Mousse back to us?"

Mom laughed and hugged me. I held on to her extra tight, glad to hear her laughing and not wanting her to be lonely anymore.

"This is a different kind of loneliness," she said finally, with a hint of embarrassment. "Maybe in a few more years we can talk about that. Now, let me straighten your bed."

Mom got up and fluffed my pillow. Then she smoothed down the blankets and tucked them up close around me—under my chin and my feet—the way she used to when I was a little girl.

"Night, Evie."

"Mom, I'll bet Mrs. Hamilton was lonely too after her husband died. Do you think that's why she got Millie?"

"Maybe."

"Do you think she stays awake at three in the morning too?"

"I wouldn't be surprised. Now, go back to sleep. I'm sorry I woke you."

"Mom?"

"Yes?"

"You're lots better than Brent's dumb old Lexus."

She smiled and bent down, tapping an index finger to my nose. "Good *night,* Evie. Don't let the bedbugs bite." Then she turned out the light.

My mother hadn't said those words to me since before Dad left.

Evie's Chewy Chocolate Chip Cookies with Pecans and Coconut

1 cup butter
2½ cups all-purpose flour
1 cup packed brown sugar
½ cup granulated sugar
2 eggs
1 teaspoon vanilla
½ teaspoon baking soda
1 twelve-ounce package semisweet
    chocolate pieces
1 cup chopped pecans
1 cup shredded coconut

🍪 Preheat oven to 375 degrees F.

🍪 In a large mixing bowl beat butter with an electric

mixer on medium to high speed for about 30 seconds, or until softened.

🍫 Add about *half* the flour to the butter. Then add brown sugar, granulated sugar, eggs, vanilla, and baking soda. Beat till thoroughly combined, scraping sides of bowl occasionally. Beat or stir in remaining flour. Stir in chocolate pieces. Then stir in nuts and coconut.

🍫 Drop dough from a rounded teaspoon 2 inches apart onto an ungreased cookie sheet. Bake for 8 to 10 minutes, or till edges are lightly browned. Remove the cookies from the cookie sheet and cool on a wire rack. Makes about 60 cookies.

Evie's Kitchen Tip #6

If you want your cookies to stay soft,
put a slice of apple in the container
before tightening the lid.

CHAPTER 7

Observation

"Anything home-baked really
personalizes a meal."
—Ann Clark

I woke up early, the sun barely clearing the edge of my window. Judging by the sounds coming from the kitchen, I figured Mom was already up. And she was trying to cook breakfast. A sure recipe for disaster.

I stretched, rolled out of bed, and bent to pick up the clothes I'd thrown on the floor last night after Karyn left. They were gone. Mom must have *really* woken early, I thought. She'd already invaded my room and snatched all the dirty laundry! Whenever she got on a roll like this, it was usually because she was angry about something. Or someone.

Glancing out the window, I caught a glimpse of Mrs. H's house and the lake shimmering beyond it. All the stuff that had happened this week still clung to me like cobwebs. Corey's nastiness in class, finding Millie and then burying her, Mom's awful date with Brent. It didn't seem right that everything continued to look the same outside. Like any other day.

I walked into the kitchen and Mom said hi without glancing up at me. I was relieved in a way, because I didn't want to see her eyes all red and puffy from blubbering over Brent. But she didn't show any signs of crying at all. She was pouring a giant glob of pancake batter into a large frying pan. And there was flour spattered everywhere. I wondered how long she'd been at this.

"Need some help?" I asked.

"I'm fine," Mom said testily.

"Okay. I'll set the table then."

"I can *handle* it, Evie," she said.

"I know you can, Mom. I only want to help, that's all."

Mom lifted her eyes to my face. They weren't pink or bloodshot, I noticed. Only tired. She looked into mine for a moment before speaking. "That would be very nice." Then she smiled, and I knew that everything was okay with her.

"How's your cooking class going?" she asked, setting one enormous oblong pancake on the table. I guess we were supposed to share it or something.

"I'm not sure," I admitted. "The teacher is sort of weird, and my cooking partner is stuck up."

Mom laughed. "Welcome to *food world*." I knew she was referring to Dad and to some of his strange friends at the newspaper. They could carry on for hours about the pros and cons of one single ingredient.

"Well, I'm armed and ready this week," I said, pointing at the enormous bag of cookies on the counter. "Nobody can resist chocolate chips with pecans and coconut."

Apparently, somebody could.

"I'm allergic to coconut," Corey said, as he set out a bowl and utensils for preparing our deviled eggs.

"Oh." I placed the unopened bag on the counter between us. "What happens when you eat it?"

He studied me strangely. Maybe no one had ever asked him that question before.

"I blow up."

For some reason this struck me as hilarious. But when I started snickering, his expression changed from perplexed to angry.

"It's not a joke," he said. "A person can die from it, you know."

"Well, yeah! I guess if your body blows up, you *would* end up dead."

He frowned, and then I saw it. A tiny twitch, tugging at one corner of his lower lip. So. Perhaps Mr. Freckle Face did have a lighter side, I thought.

Corey surveyed the row of measuring spoons in front of him and began rearranging them on the counter. "What I meant was that I puff up when I eat coconut. My face and my fingers swell, and eventually my lungs. Until I can't breathe."

"How horrible!" I said. "Has that ever happened to you? The no-breathing part, I mean?"

"Not yet," he answered. Then Corey poofed out his cheeks, crossing both eyes and letting his tongue dangle from the side of his mouth.

I laughed again. And, surprisingly, so did he.

Shanti approached our station. Today she was wearing an enormous poncho, round and woolen, like some brightly colored throw rug. "What do we have here?" she asked, observing my bag of cookies. "Something for extra credit?"

I offered her one. "No, they're just some cookies I made."

The cooking master sampled two dainty bites and cocked her head slightly. "These are quite provocative," she said. "Did you know that the word *cookie* comes from the Dutch word for 'cake'? The first cookies were actually tiny cakes, baked as a test to make sure that the oven temperature was right. But *these* tiny cakes are marvelous! Can you bring the recipe with you next time?"

"Ummm ...," I said, "it's sort of something I just made up—"

"You invented these cookies all by yourself?" Shanti was amazed.

Did I? I couldn't remember. Dad and I had been goofing around one afternoon, throwing different things into the cookie dough, but I knew that a lot of the ingredients had been thrown in by *me*.

I nodded somberly, and Shanti clapped her

hands in delight, her rows of bracelets clanking noisily.

"If you gave me a list of ingredients, could the class improvise later on? As a group project?"

"Uhhh . . . sure," I said, before she floated off to the next group. I glanced over at Corey, who was smirking at me again. "What?" I said, angrily.

"I think Shanti has a new teacher's pet."

I shifted my gaze, embarrassed. I didn't want to annoy Corey, especially if he considered himself to be the *old* teacher's pet. "Oh, I don't know. She's kind of crazy, anyway. Don't you think?"

"What do you mean?"

"Well, come on! The twirly skirts? Those bracelets, and the poncho getup? I mean, it's like Shanti never left the sixties. She's a middle-aged hippie."

"She's my aunt."

Oh, gulp! Quickly, I rewound every word of our conversation. What—exactly—had I said? And how offensive had it been? Crazy. Middle-aged. Hippie. Hmmmm. Those sounded pretty offensive, all right.

Shanti chose that moment to hold up her hand. In it she cradled a single hard-boiled egg from last week's lesson.

"The blandness of hard-cooked eggs is a challenge to all adventurous cooks," she announced enthusiastically. "And today we are *going* to be adventurous."

She instructed us to remove the yolks from our eggs and mash them in a bowl. Then Shanti handed out various moistening agents and dry spices to each of the cooking stations. Corey and I were given sweet pickle juice, sour cream, curry powder, and dry mustard. Whatever happened to plain old salt and mayonnaise?

I dipped a finger into the pickle juice and took a taste. Yikes!

"Be thankful she didn't give us anchovies and ketchup," Corey hissed, under his breath. At first, I thought that he might be irritated with me. But, to my relief, I saw that he was actually grinning.

"Did she really do that to somebody?" I asked.

"Station two," Corey said, flicking a hand in that direction. He plopped a bowl in front of me. "Come on. Pickle juice isn't so bad, once you add all the other stuff."

I pulled a spoon out of my top drawer and began mixing some of the pickle juice into my egg yolks.

"Sorry for what I said earlier. About your aunt, I mean."

Corey was mashing his own egg yolks, so I couldn't read his face. "It's okay. Shanti *is* sort of crazy sometimes."

"Is that her real name? Shanti?"

"Her original name, you mean? No. It's Betty. Betty Brightman."

I stared at him, but Corey was now refusing to make eye contact. He seemed very interested in those deviled eggs all of a sudden, and I thought I knew why.

"Betty Brightman?" I repeated. "As in *Baking with Betty*?"

Baking with Betty was an old TV show I used to watch when I was a little kid. I vaguely remembered a lady in a plaid apron and some puppets who would bother her as she worked in the kitchen. Could Shanti be this same woman?

"Yep." Corey's cheeks were now a mass of red hot freckles. Or the one cheek that I could see, anyway. And his ear glowed bright red too.

"Why did she change her name?"

"She became a Buddhist."

"Oh." I wasn't sure what to say to something like that. It sounded kind of personal.

Corey added some dry mustard to his concoction in the bowl and began stirring vigorously. "She went off to China for a couple of years," he said, "to study cooking and culture. I guess she liked Buddhism, so she converted."

"What happened to her cooking show?"

He finally focused his attention on me. "She decided to give it up."

Something in the way he said this made me think there was more to the story than he was telling. But Corey wasn't offering any explanations.

"I've seen your dad on TV," he said instead. "Without any puppets."

I chuckled. "Sometimes he lets me sit in the audience. Were you ever a guest on your aunt's show?"

"Sure, lots of times. Whenever they needed a kid to volunteer, I was always right there, planted in the front row."

Shanti drifted by just then, taking a peek over Corey's shoulder. "He was the only child in the studio who knew what a pastry blender was for," she said to me. "Here, Evie. Try a little cayenne pepper."

She sprinkled some into my bowl, then took off toward the next station.

"I forgot to tell you that Shanti has an extra set of ears and eyes in the back of her head," Corey commented with a frown.

I wondered how close the two of them really were, whether he'd go and repeat my earlier remarks about her. "Do you live with Shanti?"

He shook his head. "Are you kidding? She lives out past Route 92, on this big place that used to be a cattle ranch or something. Her and all her animals."

My ears perked up. "Animals? What kind of animals?"

"You name it. My aunt is big on rescuing injured and orphaned pets. She's got cats, dogs, rabbits, birds, hamsters, and an iguana, if you can believe that. The trouble is, she ends up keeping most of them, even after they're healthy. One of her cats had babies a couple of weeks ago, and now those kittens have taken over the entire house!"

"I used to have a dog," I said, offering him my best wistful expression. "His name was Mousse, but he sort of got taken away from me."

"Oh, my aunt's got millions of dogs too," Corey said, not looking wistful at all.

Next, Shanti instructed us to stuff the yolk fillings back into our egg whites. "Now you may all travel about the room," she added excitedly, "to sample everyone's exotic creations."

I caught Corey's eye in a panic, wondering what strange ingredients Shanti had inflicted upon her other students. At the moment, I wasn't feeling too adventurous or exotic. Maybe I should simply stay put.

"Keep away from station two," Corey warned, taking off in the opposite direction.

I watched him go, wondering if he might be such a bad cooking partner after all. Except for the allergies. And those freckles. Well. Maybe I'd bake some more cookies tonight. I could always leave out the coconut.

Shanti's Basic Deviled Eggs

6 hard-boiled eggs, peeled
¼ to ½ teaspoon salt
¼ teaspoon pepper
½ teaspoon dry mustard
3 tablespoons mayonnaise (or Miracle Whip)

Cut the eggs in half lengthwise. Slip out yolks, place them in a bowl, and mash with fork. Add salt, pepper, mustard, and mayonnaise. Stir to mix well. Refill whites with egg yolk mixture, heaping it up lightly.

Evie's Kitchen Tip #7

To keep hard-boiled eggs from getting that green ring around the yolk, use a pin to poke a tiny hole in the large end of the egg before boiling. Some say this also makes the egg easier to peel.

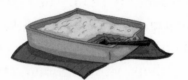

CHAPTER 8

Preparation

*"Get your windows open,
and your kitchen fan on!"*
—Emeril Lagasse

As I walked home, I saw Mrs. H, rocking on her front porch. My neighbor looked thin as a garden hose, and I wondered if she had been taking care of herself. She simply *had* to get another cat, I thought. Or a fish might be better. Something that wouldn't keep running away. But I knew a little more time had to pass first.

Mrs. Hamilton lifted her hand in a feeble wave. I suspected she'd been sitting there for a while, waiting for me.

"A storm's on the way, Evie. I can sense it. The old hip's creeking like a barn door."

I glanced up over my head. Not a cloud in the sky. In fact, the air was so quiet, it felt like the day was holding its breath. A storm? Who was she kidding? Well, I guess without Millie around, Mrs. H needed something to complain about. And someone to complain *to.*

Entering her yard, I walked up to the front porch and sat on the top step, following her gaze. The lake spread out in front of us like a shimmering blanket. It was so familiar, the one thing that never seemed to change in this town. People—and animals—could come and go, but the lake was always there, ringed with trees and silt and sand.

"I hope that ornery cat is at peace now," Mrs. Hamilton said, more to herself than to me. She was gazing at the spot under her tree where Millie now lay buried. The old woman's cheeks moved in and out slowly, as if she were chewing on something hard.

I nodded. I felt sad too, but it was a good kind of sadness now. Millie the cat was part of the earth, and out of that earth grew the cypress trees that circled the lake.

I peered at the sky again. "What do you suppose Millie's doing up there right now?"

Mrs. Hamilton let her rocking chair pick up speed. "Running away from something, most likely."

I smiled. "Maybe she's running *after* something."

Mrs. H smiled then too. "Like a bigger mouse than the last one."

"I hear they've got giant ones up in cat heaven."

She didn't say anything, but her rocking chair eased its pace a little, and a white heron swooped down and across the lake, crashing through its shiny surface in search of something tasty for lunch.

Thursday nights were Dad and Angie's birthing or Lamaze training nights at the rec center. Which meant I got to play with Mousse and spoil him rotten, while Angie practiced breathing and Dad coached her. I wondered if people had to breathe differently for twins than for other kinds of deliveries. Probably not. They just needed to breathe twice as long.

Angie answered the door. She was barefoot, and her hair was twisted into a fat braid. Without the Nikes and the power suit, she looked very young. And very pregnant.

"Oh, Evie," she said, sounding disappointed. "I was hoping it might be David."

I was surprised. "Dad's not home yet?"

"No." Angie twirled the braid around two fingers. "I'm getting kind of worried."

So was I. Angie went back inside, leaving the door open, which I decided was an invitation to follow. I entered the condo and smelled something metallic in the air. Then I noticed smoke coming from the kitchen.

"Are you cooking something—" I began.

"Oh, no! If I burned that lasagna—" Angie grabbed a hot pad, opened the oven door, and yanked out a pan of blackened pasta.

I surveyed the damage. "It's probably still okay," I said, unconvincingly.

"Open the front door, please!" she shouted, rushing past me to place the sizzling lasagna on the stoop. Angie walked back in, slamming the door behind her and hastily making her way toward the kitchen.

"Another one bites the dust," she said, a hint of amusement crossing her features.

I inhaled, then coughed. I wasn't sure what to do.

"Shouldn't we open some windows or something? You know . . . to clear out the smoke?"

Angie blinked. "I guess."

She made no move to crack open a window, so I reached behind her to unlatch the one above the kitchen sink.

"So, you were making dinner?" I asked. Well, duh.

"Attempting to," she replied, plopping herself in a chair and extending both legs. Angie's belly was enormous. In a single month it had inflated, like a giant beach ball stuffed inside her dress.

"Should you even *be* cooking?" I said.

Angie's air was one of disdain. "Oh, pleeeze!" she said. "You sound exactly like David. I'm not dying, you know. Just pregnant."

I pulled out a chair and sat down too. "With twins," I reminded her.

"Don't I know it!" Angie sighed. "I can't stand up, I can't sit down, I can't sleep, I can't walk. And I truly don't think I will ever be able to see my own feet again!"

I couldn't help it. I cracked up. To my surprise, Angie did too.

"It was a new recipe," she said, gesturing in the direction of her lasagna out on the stoop. "A surprise for your father."

I thought about Angie, huge and uncomfortable and all alone in this beautiful condominium, attempting to cook a flawless meal for my perfectionist father. And I was suddenly uncomfortable too. No, no, no. This felt all wrong, sympathizing with my stepmother. Sympathizing with Angie, for crying out loud!

But it was hard not to. I knew exactly what she was going through. Nothing anyone *else* cooked was ever quite good enough for my father. And he usually let them know it. My mother had never wanted to set foot in the kitchen, so cooking was not an issue for her. But what if it was for Angie?

Well, of course it was. She had been Dad's cooking editor, after all. How could you write about food, if you couldn't prepare it?

As if reading my mind, Angie slapped both hands down on the table. "So now you know, Evie," she said defiantly. "I can't cook. I am a disaster in the kitchen. And I'm married to Carson's Cuisine!"

Angie was a lot of things, but a whiner was not

one of them. Even now, she wasn't asking for pity. She was purely and plainly disgusted with herself.

"I've been collecting recipes for months," she moaned, "waiting for the perfect evening, the perfect dinner." Angie glanced over at the front door again. "Well, I guess this isn't going to be that dinner."

"Maybe I can help you," I said, immediately wishing I could take the words back and swallow them whole.

Angie contemplated me with interest. "You would do that?" she said, finally. And it struck me for the first time that my father's wife didn't trust me any more than I did her. Was this some sort of a test? Had Dad planned to leave the two of us alone again? But how could that be? He knew nothing about his wife's lasagna dinner. And besides, he and Angie were supposed to have left for their Lamaze class already.

"What in the—" We could hear feet stomping outside the front door and a few choice words coming from my father.

"Oh, my God!" Angie exclaimed. "The lasagna!" Then, inexplicably, she began to laugh. Or maybe not so inexplicably. The thought of my dad scraping gooey pasta off his shoes, outside in the dark, was really very funny. I started laughing too.

The door opened, and my father walked in, holding his shoes in one hand. Red meat sauce dripped from the soles. Mousse went crazy, of course, although I wasn't sure if his excitement was due to Dad's arrival or the shoes being juggled over his head. He jumped onto my father's legs, trying to get at them. Then, smelling the sauce on Dad's trousers, Mousse settled for licking the cuffs of my father's pants instead. I peeked over at Angie, and the two of us started laughing all over again.

Dad was trying to shake the dog off his leg. Neither of them appeared to be pleased.

"Can someone tell me why a charred concoction was out on the front stoop, where no one could possibly avoid stepping in it?" he shouted.

Angie's gaiety immediately subsided, and she studied me anxiously.

This is it, I thought. I should simply announce the truth about Angie's cooking skills. Right now. Then my father could scold his wife, and I'd be free to go home and tell Mom all about it. My mother would be busting up over this one for weeks too, knowing that Angie—the fabulous food editor—didn't know a whisk from a waffle iron.

But then Angie would undoubtedly hate me. My dad's new wife might never forgive me, and I'd have to live with it. Oh, gulp. Here I was, stuck between both families again, and not sure where I fit in.

"*I* left the lasagna out there," I blurted, before Angie could open her mouth. Angie's stare bored into me, but she didn't barge in with the real story. So I went on. "I thought I'd try out this new recipe . . . while you guys were at your Lamaze class."

Dad gazed at the mess in his left hand. "This is lasagna?"

I shrugged. "Well, it was."

I could tell that he wanted to yell at me. Really yell. But with Angie here, I guess he thought better of it. Setting the pan and his shoes in the sink, my father came over and kissed his wife on the top of the head instead.

"So . . . how's my girl?" he said.

"Fine," we both answered at the same time, and then gaped at each other, astonished. Dad seemed embarrassed. So was I, for that matter. I realized instantly that his question had been meant for Angie and not for me. After all, I was only a visitor here.

Then Angie did something unexpected. She reached over and wrapped one of her hands around mine. She looked up at Dad and grinned. "We're both fine, David," she said. "*Both* of your girls are just fine."

I knew this declaration was Angie's way of thanking me for coming to her rescue. And maybe she was letting me know I really was welcome here too, that I wasn't merely the pesky kid who showed up on Lamaze nights. I still felt stuck, though, and I wasn't quite sure how to deal with that. I had lied to my dad to cover for his wife, and to keep peace with my family on this side of the lake.

But my mother on the other side would not be

happy to learn of this tentative new truce with Angie. Which meant I'd be lying again, to keep peace with Mom now too.

Jeez! Living this double life was almost like being a referee at a soccer match.

Angie's Beef Lasagna

1½ pounds ground round or sirloin
¼ teaspoon garlic powder
2 tablespoons dried parsley flakes
1 tablespoon dried basil
2 teaspoons salt
2 (14.5-ounce) cans diced tomatoes
2 (6-ounce) cans tomato paste
10 ounces lasagna noodles, cooked
1½ pounds mozzarella cheese, sliced thin
4 cups ricotta cheese
2 eggs, beaten
½ teaspoon ground black pepper
1 cup grated Parmesan cheese

Brown meat slowly in heavy skillet. Add garlic powder, *half* of the parsley, the basil, *half* of the salt, the tomatoes, and the tomato paste. Simmer uncovered on low heat about 30 minutes, stirring occasionally. Meanwhile, follow package directions to cook noodles in large pot of boiling salted water until tender. Drain and rinse in cold water.

🍃 Preheat oven to 375 degrees F. Spray a large lasagna pan with no-stick spray. In large bowl, combine ricotta with beaten eggs, pepper, grated Parmesan, and the remaining parsley and salt. When meat sauce is ready, begin assembling lasagna.

🍃 Place a layer of cooked noodles on bottom of pan. Spread half of cheese mixture over it. Add layer of mozzarella slices. Top with half of meat sauce. Repeat all 4 layers. When assembled, you may cover with foil and refrigerate until ready to bake, or bake immediately for 30 minutes. Let stand about 10 minutes before cutting.

🍃 Serves 6–8.

Evie's Kitchen Tip #8
To take any bitterness out of your meat sauce, add a spoonful of grape jelly.

CHAPTER 9

Temperature

"It can be hard to control the heat."
—Bobby Flay

Week number four, and Corey still hadn't complimented me about my cooking. Or about anything else, for that matter. Today his aunt wore a gauzy wrap-around skirt, and her hair was swept up into some kind of colorful turban.

"Baking today," Corey informed me. "Muffins, I think."

"Oh," I said, instantly relieved. Not much you could do to mess up muffins.

"Attention, class," Shanti said, her fingers raised

in the now familiar gesture, calling us to order. "Today we are baking muffins, although each station will be following a slightly different recipe."

She proceeded to pass out instructions and ingredients to each group of students. As she did so, Corey leaned over and whispered to me.

"One of my aunt's orphans had puppies last night."

"Puppies!" I gasped. I immediately thought of my mother. Would she let me have a brand-new puppy, I wondered? A friend for Mousse? Well, why not? A pet might benefit her too. Maybe with a warm, fuzzy new puppy in the house, Mom could stop being so lonely at three o'clock in the morning.

"Will Shanti be keeping all of them, or giving some away, do you think?"

"Don't know," Corey said. "You want one?"

Before I could answer, Shanti dropped a recipe onto our counter. I read the top line: "Blueberry Muffins with Granola Topping." Weird. But how could you go wrong with blueberry muffins?

"First, we must preheat our ovens," Shanti announced from the center of the room. "Although *preheat* is a nonsensical term, if you stop to analyze it. We are simply heating the ovens to a certain temperature, not *pre*heating them at all."

We stared at her, not quite getting it.

"Never mind," she said quickly. "Just turn your ovens on and set the temperature according to your instructions."

Corey was already fiddling with the oven knobs.

I surveyed the list of ingredients. "You're not allergic to blueberries too, are you?" I asked him.

"As a matter of fact, I am," he said seriously. "I turn blue."

I wasn't sure he was joking, until he pretended to choke. Then I slugged him in the arm.

Shanti came around to each station, showing us how to cream the sugar into the butter. "This is a very important step," she told us. "No one wants lumpy muffins. Or lumpy cakes or cookies, for that matter."

Next, we added the flour and the other dry ingredients to the mix, and began stirring. Corey and I took turns with a large wooden spoon.

"I *do* want a puppy," I said to Corey, when his aunt was out of earshot. "Do you think she'll let me have one?"

"Don't know," Corey said again. "You'll have to ask her."

While the muffins were cooking, we decided to scour the sink and clean the dishes we had used.

"Your dad writes cookbooks, doesn't he?" Corey asked, as he wiped down the counter with a wet rag.

"Yeah. He's doing a series called Urban Eating in the Suburbs. All ethnic and health stuff. Your aunt would love it."

Corey groaned. "Just what Shanti needs. More recipes. She tests them all on me and my brother to make sure they won't kill anyone."

Smiling, I said, "Well, you're not dead yet."

He twirled the dishrag a couple of times. "So . . . do you want to be a writer too?" he asked me.

"No. How about you?"

"I think I might. Not cookbooks, though. Travel books. I want to travel and photograph wild habitats, maybe help protect endangered areas, like the rain forests."

"Oh." This was more than Corey had ever revealed to me. "Well, I hope you do."

Corey was silent for a while, wiping the same

spot on the counter over and over again. Finally, he said, "But don't tell anybody about it, okay?"

I was surprised. "I won't, if you don't want me to. Have you told anyone else?"

He shook his head.

"You mean, you've never talked to anybody at all about this? Not even Shanti?"

"Nope."

This made me feel funny inside, knowing that I was somehow the guardian of what Corey dreamed of doing. And I instantly wondered if he wanted to take it back. Maybe he'd made an unexpected leap— letting his secret out like that—and then regretted revealing so much of himself to someone he barely knew. Wow. First Angie's secret, now his. I must look very trustworthy or something.

"So . . . I'm the *first* one to know?"

"I guess so." He appeared as surprised as I was. "What about you? What do you want to do?"

"I'd like to be a chef," I answered immediately, then made a face. "Stupid, huh?"

"No, I think you'd make a good chef," he said, grinning at me. "But you need to learn how to cook first."

He grabbed a couple of oven mitts, pulled the muffins out, and set them on the counter. There was a smudge of flour on his cheek, but he was too intent on his task to notice.

"I'd like to enter something into the photography contest at the art museum," Corey said. "But I have to get some new lenses first, for close-ups and stuff."

We pried the muffins from the tin and began piling them on a rack.

"Do you have lots of pictures? Ones that you've taken, I mean?"

"Oh, yeah, lots." Hmmm. This guy seemed to be good at nearly everything. Which explained why he thought I was totally incompetent. But he *did* say I'd make a good chef. . . .

Shanti arrived and peered over Corey's shoulder. She plucked a muffin off the rack and nibbled on it thoughtfully. "Not bad," she said. Then to me, Shanti added, "I hear you'd like to have a replacement puppy."

Corey was hiding a smile. I didn't know he'd said anything to his aunt about my misplaced dog! Well, not misplaced, exactly. But Mousse was certainly not in my possession any longer.

"Only if you can spare one," I said quickly.

"Well, they are all too tiny to leave their mother just yet. But a number of people are driving over next week to see them. Maybe you could come take a look too, if you'd like. Pick one out for yourself."

I nearly threw my arms around her neck and kissed her. "You mean it? I can really have one?" Now . . . if I could only convince Mom. Then I had another thought. Perhaps it was time for Mrs. Hamilton to get another pet, as well. This might be the very shove she needed.

"Can I bring a friend with me? She needs a new cat."

"Certainly," Shanti said, arms waving and jewelry clanking. "A home for every animal and an animal for every home. That's my motto."

She took off toward the next cooking station, and I turned to Corey. "My neighbor just lost her cat," I explained, "and I want to convince her to come with me. Maybe Mrs. Hamilton will see one that she likes."

Corey's forehead crinkled. "Some people don't want to get a new pet when their old one dies," he said. "They think the new one will never be as good as the one they had."

"I know," I admitted, "but a new pet is just what she needs, to cheer her up."

"Have you asked your neighbor about this yet?"

"Not exactly. . . ."

He let out a hoot.

"It's not funny," I said, defensively. "Mrs. Hamilton is really bad about accepting help. And if she thought I was doing this for *her*, then she'd refuse to come with me. So I have to get her there without letting her know that's what I'm doing."

"Sounds complicated."

"It is."

Shanti came around once more to make sure that everyone's stations were cleaned up. She quickly dismissed us all, but not before handing Corey a mop. "Could you pick up all the dish towels for me today, Evie?" she asked.

I made my way around the room, snatching towels and rags from countertops. Shanti took them from me with a great big smile. "You *must* come meet my newest dog. He's a dear," she said. Then, leaning closer, she added, "Except for his unhealthy obsession with squirrels."

"His name is Trooper," Corey stated, passing the dirty mop back to his aunt. "His latest name anyway."

Shanti grunted, shoving the dirty towels into a plastic bag. "Poor thing's been abandoned by two owners and had his name changed more times than that," she said, clearly in disbelief. Then her eyes warmed. "But Trooper is beautiful. His coat is the color of caramel corn, and his fur is soft as chenille."

"So why would anybody abandon him?" I asked.

Shanti shot a glance at Corey, but he was staring at the floor.

"Cancer," she said. "Inoperable. Trooper is dying."

"What!" I couldn't understand why anyone would desert a sick dog. Or why someone else would adopt him, only to watch him grow sicker.

"His death sentence was just the latest excuse for his owners to turn their backs on him," Shanti said. "I heard about Trooper nineteen days ago, through the Canine Underground Railroad."

I listened to her, spellbound. A Canine Underground Railroad? I'd never heard of such a thing.

"A friend of mine who does animal rescue

e-mailed me. Trooper was about to be put to sleep, and Glenda said she had a CUR run coming up that weekend, and she could pull the dog out for me if I wanted him."

"And of course Shanti wanted him," Corey added, as if it were the most natural thing in the world for his aunt to order a sick dog over the Internet. Then again, maybe it was.

"Everybody wants the *perfect* dog," Shanti said, making her way toward the door as Corey and I followed. "Nobody wants the ones that are maimed. But those are the animals I want. Because they deserve to be loved that much more."

She walked to her car, an old Volkswagen van adorned with faded daisies, and threw the mop and bag of towels into the back.

"I hope you'll come to see us, Evie," she said, climbing in and motioning Corey into the passenger side. "And bring your friend!"

Corey slid into his seat, and Shanti drove off. I watched the van rumble away, followed by a fan of exhaust fumes and swirling gray dust.

Evie & Corey's Blueberry Muffins with Granola Topping

MUFFIN MIXTURE:

2 cups sugar

1 cup butter, melted

4 cups all-purpose flour

2 cups sour cream

1 (10-ounce) bag frozen blueberries
(do not thaw)

½ teaspoon baking soda

2 teaspoons baking powder

1 teaspoon salt

4 eggs

GRANOLA MIXTURE:

¼ cup granola

1 tablespoon brown sugar

1 tablespoon butter, softened

¼ teaspoon pumpkin pie spice

🍇 Preheat oven to 375 degrees F. Grease the muffin tins or line them with cupcake papers.

🍇 Using a wooden spoon, cream sugar into melted butter in a large bowl until mixture is pale and creamy and drops off spoon easily. Combine with rest of muffin mixture ingredients; do not overmix. Spoon into muffin tins.

🍇 Combine granola mixture ingredients, mixing well. Sprinkle on top of each muffin. Bake for 25 minutes. Makes 12 muffins.

Evie's Kitchen Tip #9

To keep muffins from burning around the edges, leave one muffin cup empty and fill ⅔ with cold water before baking.

CHAPTER 10

Anticipation

"There are a million things you can do in advance to make cooking less stressful."
—Ina Garten, the Barefoot Contessa

Mom was in the kitchen, attempting to fix herself some lunch. She wore faded blue jeans, and her hair was pulled back into two uneven pigtails. Good. No more purple eyelids for any of her piano parents.

"How was class today?" she asked, trying unsuccessfully to peel what appeared to be a mutilated cucumber.

"Okay, I guess. We made muffins. Do you need a hand with that?"

My mother motioned to a chopping block filled

with fresh vegetables. "How about helping me with this salad?"

I snatched a knife from the dishwasher and began slicing some mushrooms. "Turns out that Shanti, my cooking master, used to be Betty Brightman," I said, thinking I'd ease slowly into the subject of getting a new dog.

Mom set her cucumber down with a thump. "You mean, *Baking with Betty*?"

"Yep."

"Where has she been all this time?"

"Traveling. China, mostly. She's a Buddhist now."

My mother stared at me. I was not getting any closer to a new dog.

"And she sort of runs a pet shelter, out near Route 92. As part of the Canine Underground Railroad."

Mom's expression said it all. Her daughter was taking a cooking class from a nut job.

"It's really okay, Mom. Shanti isn't a freak or anything like that. She just loves animals."

Mom picked up the cucumber again. "And how do you know about all of this?"

"Her nephew Corey is my cooking partner." Here goes, I thought. Might as well jump right in. "He told me that his aunt has some new puppies and that I can have one, if I want."

My mother sighed and dropped her knife. "Oh, Evie, I don't know. . . ."

"You said yourself that you're lonely. A new dog could keep you company when I'm not at home."

"A new dog could chew up all the furniture and pee on the carpet when *I'm* not at home."

I bit my tongue.

"Look, I know you're not happy about this. But I really don't have time to house train a puppy."

"You wouldn't have to. I'll do everything!"

"What about when school starts in the fall? Who will take care of the dog then?"

"You didn't used to talk this way about *Mousse*!" I shouted.

"Mousse was your father's dog. Not mine."

There it was again. *Your father.* She made the words sound dirty or something. And besides, Mom was wrong about Mousse. That dog had been just as much mine as he'd been Dad's.

"Oh, forget it," I said angrily. "Just forget I even asked." I stalked out of the kitchen and into my room, where I flopped down on my unmade bed. This wasn't about a new dog at all, I thought. It was about Dad. About the two of them haggling over what was his and what was hers.

Again.

I showed up early to walk Mousse that Thursday. Mom had scheduled a five-o'clock piano lesson, so I grabbed my opportunity to leave the house without having to talk to her about taking care of dogs—new ones *or* old ones.

Angie answered the door, wearing a red-and-white-checked apron. "Oh, hi, Evie. Aren't you kind of early? I wasn't expecting you until six."

"Yeah. Well. I thought maybe I'd hang around here for a while."

Her eyebrows rose, but she didn't ask anything more.

"Where's Mousse?" I said.

As if on cue, the enormous dog bounded through the living room, his broad tail barely missing a china vase on the coffee table. Mousse jumped up on me, lapping my face, and Angie laughed.

"If he did that to me, I'd fall over backward and have to lie there until David got home to hoist me up." She pointed to her protuding belly. "Low center of gravity, and getting lower every day."

I stroked Mousse gently, forcing his front paws down. "When are the babies actually due?"

"Six more weeks." She groaned. "But twins usually come early. Too crowded in there."

I knew the feeling. "How's the cooking going?" I asked. I'd actually brought a recipe along with me to give to Angie. Roast lamb with plum sauce, one of Dad's favorites.

"Better," she replied. "At least nothing has ended up outside the front door again. Hey, I made a lemon meringue pie this morning. Want a piece?" She started toward the kitchen, and I followed her, Mousse frolicking behind me. He could always sense when people were making their way toward food.

Angie cut two slices of pie and set them on the table. "I guess I'll have to go on a diet after the babies come, but for now the doctor keeps telling me to eat. And believe me, I've been eating."

We chewed in silence for a while, then Angie suddenly stopped, the fork halfway to her mouth.

"You know something, Evie? I have absolutely no

idea how to take care of a baby. And now I'm having *two* of them."

"Don't they teach you that kind of stuff in your Lamaze classes?"

Angie laughed humorlessly. "Are you kidding? They teach you how to breathe and how to push. Then they send you home from the hospital with a blanket and some diapers and these two new little *people* that you don't even know, and you're suddenly on your own. Bye-bye! Have a happy rest of your life."

I thought about the two dolls I used to play with, only a few years ago. Gina and Tina, I'd named them. Where were they now? In the back of my closet somewhere. I'd abandoned those naked babies the minute I grew tired of changing them and burping them. But real babies, now. That was a whole differ-ent story. Like Angie said, they were little people. No wonder she was so scared.

"Dad will help you," I said, knowing that this was true. Although my father had divorced my mother, I knew enough to admit that he'd always been there for me. Taken me to dance lessons and swim lessons—and to countless powwows during my Indian princess phase. The two of us had made so many leather belts, we wove them all together into one long dog leash for Mousse.

"Oh, I know that," Angie said quickly. "David's been wonderful. It's still scary, though. And it's funny, don't you think? In the pioneer days, there were always other family members around to share in the child rearing. I mean, mothers and aunts and grandmothers. Everyone was always *there*, you know? Not like nowadays, with people so spread out. It seems like we're going backward sometimes, doesn't it?"

I had no answer to that. My aunt Tricia lived miles from Clermont Lake, and I kind of liked it that way. "*I'm* here," I said, instantly feeling as frightened as Angie was. Let's face it. What did I know about babies? I certainly couldn't breathe and push.

Angie cocked her head, just barely. She seemed to be weighing my offer. "Well, that you are," she said finally.

By the time I got home, Mom's music lessons were done and she was sitting in the living room listening to music.

"Mozart?" I asked, taking a stab at conversation.

We'd been sort of prickly with each other ever since the no-dog argument, and I missed talking with her. But I was still angry about the puppy. And I still wanted one.

Mom answered, "Chopin. One of his études."

I stood there uncomfortably. My mother patted a spot on the sofa next to her, and I sat down reluctantly, hands folded in my lap.

"I'm sorry about what I said earlier," Mom admitted. "About Mousse only being your father's dog. I know he was yours too. That's why you'd like another dog."

"I don't want to replace him—" I began.

"You want something of your own," she said. "I know. And I'm sorry."

I brightened. "Does that mean I can get a puppy after all?"

Mom put a hand on my folded ones. "It means I'll think about it. How does that sound?"

It sounded pretty lame to me, but I knew better than to argue the point, now that I'd sort of won her over to my side. "Okay, I guess."

She smiled. "Good."

"Do you think Mrs. Hamilton might want a pet too?" I said. "I thought I might ask her."

"Oh, I think she's a little too old to deal with a puppy. They can be pretty spunky."

"No, no. I was thinking about another cat. Do you think she'd like a kitten?"

"That might work, but you'd have to convince her to take a look at one first."

I'd thought this out already, but I wasn't sure if Mom would go for it. "What if I told her that I was going to pick out a dog for myself and asked her to come along, to help me choose? And . . . if she just happens to see a cat she can't resist. . . ."

Mom threw her hands up in surrender. "Then I think I'd better come too, before you end up bringing Betty Brightman's entire pet population home with you."

"You promise? Shanti said a lot of people will be there next week, picking their favorites."

"I'm not promising anything, but you can talk to Mrs. Hamilton tomorrow, okay?"

Mom got up off the couch to choose another CD, and then she turned to me, almost shyly. "Would you like to watch a movie before dinner? I checked one out this afternoon. A real tearjerker."

"Did you buy extra Kleenex?" I asked.

"Two boxes."

"It's a date," I said, grinning, then I ran to my room before she could change her mind about the dog.

Upstairs, I couldn't help sifting through the closet for Gina and Tina, my abandoned "babies" from years ago. There they were, still naked as anything, with their bald heads and fluttering lashes. I felt guilty for shoving them under my discarded sneakers and sweatshirts. Even if they were just dolls, they deserved better treatment. So I set them side by side on my dresser, covering them with one of my old sweatshirts. Then I ran downstairs to watch that weepy movie with my mom.

Angie's Creamy Lemon Meringue Pie

1 large lemon
1 cup plus 2 teaspoons sugar
Pinch salt
¼ cup plus 1 heaping teaspoon cornstarch
1½ cups cold water
4 eggs, separated
1 tablespoon butter
1 well-baked 9-inch pie crust
Pinch cream of tartar

🍮 Preheat oven to 375 degrees F. Grate the zest from the lemon and set aside; juice lemon and set aside.

In medium saucepan combine the cup of sugar, salt, and cornstarch. Gradually stir in water until smooth. Beat egg yolks slightly, using wire whisk, then add them to pan. Stirring constantly, bring to boil over medium heat and boil 1 minute. Remove from heat. Stir in lemon zest, lemon juice, and butter. Spoon hot filling onto crust, then gently smooth top.

In small mixer bowl, beat egg whites at high speed until foamy. Gradually beat in cream of tartar and remaining 2 teaspoons sugar until stiff peaks form. Spoon meringue on top of hot filling, starting at outside edge, and continue into center. Bake for 5 minutes, then reduce oven to 350 degrees F. for 10 to 15 minutes. Rotate pie every 5 minutes to make sure it browns evenly.

Cool on wire rack, then refrigerate until cold before serving. Makes 8 servings.

Evie's Kitchen Tip #10

If you want the best volume for whipped egg whites, select smaller eggs. Smaller eggs have less water content and the white is more concentrated.

CHAPTER 11

Simplification

*"Simplicity is one of the most fundamental
keys to preparing food well."*
—Mario Batali

Now that Millie the cat had been gone for more than a month, there was no obvious reason for Mrs. H to call me anymore. I can't say that I minded, and I certainly didn't miss searching for an animal who had no intention of being found. But I wondered how Mrs. Hamilton was doing. I hadn't seen her on the porch or in the yard for days, and it worried me.

The next evening, I decided to walk across her lawn with a plate of brownies and ask her about coming with us to Shanti's house. As usual, there was no answer when I knocked on the front door. Mrs. Hamilton's faulty hearing, I thought. Another good reason for that woman to own a pet. An animal could alert her to houseguests, not to mention burglars.

"Mrs. Hamilton?" I slipped inside and crept across the living room, not wanting to startle her. A light was on in the kitchen, and I figured she was either eating or cleaning up after supper.

The room was empty, the table and counters wiped spotless. There was a stillness to the place that was eerie, as if no one lived here anymore. Then, from under the sink, I spied two motionless legs, their toes pointed down and out, like a ballet dancer's. A wave of panic washed over me. Had Mrs. H fallen again? Was she dead?

"Mrs. Hamilton!" I said again, only much

louder this time, and the legs gave a start, as if I had poked them with a red-hot stick.

"Ouch!" The limbs scooted toward me, and Mrs. H emerged from under her kitchen sink, scowling. When she saw me, the scowl deepened. "Evie, what in heaven's name are you doing, sneaking around my house in the middle of the night?"

I glanced at my watch. It was only eight o'clock. Helplessly, I held out the plate of brownies, and her features softened a little.

"Well, why didn't you say so? Put them on the table, and I'll get us some ice cream to go with them." She motioned for me to help her up off the floor.

"What were you doing under there?" I asked as she washed her hands.

"Fixing the drain," she said. "Darn thing's got a leak." A year ago Mrs. H could have asked my father to come over and fix something like that for her. And I wondered why she hadn't at least called me.

"You know how to do that?" I said, surprised.

"Used to work on pipes all the time, during the war," she replied, placing two bowls and two spoons on the table. "Had a job as a plumber while Gus served overseas."

Something else I'd never known about my next-door neighbor. I don't think I'd have been more surprised if Mrs. Hamilton had informed me she was once an acrobat in the circus.

I sat down and we ate, chewing wordlessly for a while. It was odd, not having Millie yowling at us from under the table. And I didn't know what to say to my neighbor, now that neither one of us could complain about our animals.

"Your kitchen is different," I said at last, noticing that the floor was no longer strewn with cat food bowls.

"Oh, I've been straightening up a bit," Mrs. H said, "now that Millie's gone."

Here was my chance to talk her into a new pet, I thought. But how would I start?

"I miss Mousse sometimes," I began. "That's why I'm thinking of getting another dog."

She studied me curiously. "Why would you want to do that?"

I thought I'd just *told* her why. "Because I miss Mousse," I repeated.

Mrs. H waved a hand toward the lapping water only a few steps beyond her front porch. "But you can go to the other side of the lake and see him any-time you want."

This was true, but visiting Mousse was not the same as having him here with me all the time. I missed him lying on my bed while I read my cook-books and gobbling up crumbs from the floor after I'd finished baking.

"He's not really mine anymore," I said.

Mrs. H nodded sadly and stopped eating her ice cream. I went on. "But a friend of mine has an aunt who works for the Canine Underground Railroad and she—"

Her face snapped to attention. "The what?"

I told her about Shanti who had befriended a sick dog named Trooper over the Internet. Mrs. Hamil-ton seemed interested. "People can actually rescue animals who are dying?" she asked.

"I guess so," I responded. "Anyway, Shanti has a house full of them. Animals, I mean. Not all of them are dying, though. I think most of them are sick or abandoned. She nurses them back to health and tries to find homes for them." I emphasized the word *homes*, hoping that Mrs. H would take the hint.

Instead, she grew wary. "Sounds like hard work to me," she grumbled. "And pointless."

Oh, gulp. This was not going as planned.

"So," I continued quickly, "I'm going over there next week to see a litter of new puppies, and I thought maybe you'd like to come with me."

"Whatever for?" she exclaimed.

I leaned forward, elbows on the table. "To help me pick one out. I mean, it's a big decision. Pets are serious business."

Mrs. Hamilton's eyes focused on mine. They were moist and half closed, surrounded by lines as interwoven as a spider's web. Now they suddenly crinkled shut, the corners of her mouth curving upward, and I knew she was thinking about Millie.

"They certainly are," she agreed, her head bobbing up and down as if it were dangling from an invisible string.

And I knew—just like that—she'd be coming with me.

"We're going to Shanti's," I whispered to Corey as we began peeling apples for our pie filling. His freckles appeared almost purple next to his bright magenta

T-shirt, which said, PHOTOGRAPHERS ARE FLASHY. And his eyes shone, clear and ice-blue. Why hadn't I ever paid attention to the color before? Shoot! I was staring at him. I attacked my apple with extra energy, cutting it into fourths.

"We?" he repeated.

I was coring the apple now. "My mom's coming. And Mrs. Hamilton too."

He let out a low whistle. "It's a good thing Maggie had a large litter." Then he grimaced. "Shanti thinks one of them might be blind, though."

My heart did a little double beat, and I met his gaze. "Blind? How can she tell?"

Corey shrugged. "I guess he's having trouble finding where Maggie's milk is coming from."

I couldn't imagine how a blind dog might ever survive in this world. Would it have to be put to sleep? No. I didn't think Shanti could do that. Not if she went around rescuing dogs with inoperable cancer.

Shanti appeared at the cooking station right then, to examine our progress. Her hair was loose today, silver tendrils flying every which way. She had a bright red scarf knotted around her neck, and the bracelets on her arms jangled as she deposited some brown sugar and cinnamon on the counter.

"Will you be coming over for a puppy, Evie?" Shanti asked me in that breathy, urgent voice of hers.

"Yes, if that's all right. I'm bringing my mom and my neighbor too."

The cooking master beamed. "Lovely! Do you know how to get there?"

"No."

"Just take Marshall all the way out to County Road 510. Then take a right on Route 92 and look for the white two-story house on the left. My van should be in the driveway."

I nodded, hoping I'd remember all of that for Mom later. Shanti glided off before I could ask her about the blind puppy. My apples were peeled, so I began chopping them into small chunks.

"Will you be there too?" I asked Corey, hoping that I didn't sound too eager. Why should he be there anyway?

Corey stood next to me, motionless except for his jaw, which kept moving around and around, like he was chewing on a bag of marbles.

"Don't know," he said finally. "Would you like me to be?"

I didn't dare sneak a peek at him, afraid that he'd be smirking at me. Or worse, frowning.

"Yes," I managed.

He resumed his chopping, although I noticed that the apple chunks in front of him were already smaller than lentils. "Okay, then," he said, and his face flushed, clear down to the neckline of his T-shirt.

I tried to hide my smile as I dumped both our piles of decimated apple into the bowl.

Yes!

Evie & Corey's Hot Apple Pie

REFRIGERATED EGG PASTRY
(makes enough for 2 or 3 double crusts):
5 cups unsifted all-purpose flour
1 teaspoon salt
1 teaspoon baking powder
2 cups butter or canola oil
1 egg, beaten
1 teaspoon white vinegar
Ice water

🍎 Blend flour, salt, baking powder, and shortening with a pastry blender to a mealy consistency. Mix the beaten egg with vinegar; add enough ice water to make 1 cup liquid. Make a well in the dry ingredients and add just enough liquid to form a dough. Mix with a fork and add liquid gradually; you may not need it all. Form dough into two or three balls; roll in waxed paper or plastic wrap, and chill in the refrigerator.

> *PIE FILLING:*
> *12 to 15 green apples such as Granny Smith*
>   *(about 8 cups sliced)*
> *2 tablespoons lemon juice*
> *½ cup granulated sugar*
> *½ cup brown sugar*
> *½ teaspoon salt*
> *1 teaspoon cinnamon*
> *½ teaspoon nutmeg*
> *2 tablespoons flour*
> *2 tablespoons butter*

🍎 Preheat oven to 450 degrees F. Peel, core, and slice apples (not too thin) into a large bowl. Add lemon juice to keep from browning. Toss with sugars, salt, spices, and flour.

🍎 Cut a ball of pastry in half and roll out one half to form bottom crust; line deep-dish pie plate. Arrange apples in crust. Dot with small pieces of the butter. Roll out top crust pastry and cover pie with it. Crimp edges together; cut slits in top crust to allow steam to escape. Place on baking pan to catch juices that bubble over. Put in pre-heated oven; immediately reduce heat to 350 degrees F. Bake for about 1 hour or until crust is just golden brown and juices bubbling over. Cool to room temperature before serving. Makes 1 deep-dish pie.

Evie's Kitchen Tip #11

To keep baked edges of your pie crust from getting too brown, cover the edges with foil after the first fifteen minutes.

CHAPTER 12

Diversity

*"Serve hot food on hot plates,
and cold food on cold plates."*
—Sara Moulton

Dad had promised that I could pick out the restaurant for our July snob dinner, so I chose Tortini's. It was my favorite Italian restaurant, mainly because Mr. Tortini always gave us extra bread sticks. I think he was hoping that my father would mention the restaurant in his column or on TV. So far that hadn't happened. But the bread sticks just kept on coming.

"So," Dad said, after our food had arrived, "are you enjoying your cooking class?"

"It's okay," I said, trying not to sound too enthusiastic. "Our teacher is Betty Brightman."

Dad threw his head back and laughed. "The lady with the puppets?"

"Well, yeah," I said. "But she really is a good teacher. And she doesn't use puppets anymore."

"I'm sure she's terrific, pumpkin seed. To tell you the truth, I've often wondered what happened to her."

I dug into my linguini with clam sauce. "Oh, she became a Buddhist."

Dad looked at me, his fork hovering above his plate.

"And now she teaches cooking classes and rescues injured pets. In fact, Mom and I are going over to her house later this week to look at some of her puppies."

He chewed thoughtfully, then set his fork back down. "I'll let you in on a little secret about Betty Brightman," he said. "She could have been big. Published her own cookbooks. Starred in her own nationally syndicated TV show. The works."

I was surprised. "Why didn't she?"

Dad shrugged. "I guess fame wasn't Betty's thing.

One day, without any warning, she just left." He paused. "And then I stepped in."

That would have been right before my sixth birthday, I thought. Dad gave up his full-time job at the newspaper around then so that he could start his own TV show. But I'd never known it was Shanti's spot he was taking. And I wondered if this bothered her at all. Maybe that's why Corey had clammed up that day when I'd asked about his aunt's television career.

Weird. All of us seemed to be intertwined somehow. Dad took over Shanti's TV show, then she became my cooking instructor, then her nephew became my cooking partner, and now my mother and Mrs. Hamilton were going to take a look at her animals. One single thread, connecting us all. I thought Shanti would approve of that idea.

"I'll tell you one thing. You're learning from a real pro," Dad said, then he stopped. "You *are* learning, aren't you?"

"Yes." I laughed. "I'm learning a lot."

"Good. Then I'll be expecting a sample when the class is over," he said.

"Should it be perfect?" I asked, grinning. After all,

that was the purpose of our snob dinners. To find the imperfections in every possible meal.

"*Nearly* perfect," Dad said, and smiled. "That's plenty good enough."

Yeah, right. Nearly perfect was nearly impossible, where my father was concerned. I swallowed loudly, wondering if he could hear it, but Dad was studying the menu again.

"Now, what should we order for dessert, Evie?"

Karyn and I went swimming a couple of days later. Her apartment complex had a giant pool, with a diving board and a water slide. Afterward, we sat on a couple of green plastic lounge chairs, trying to get a tan.

"How's the cooking class going?" Karyn said, squinting at me. It was pretty much the same question my Dad had asked, only I knew she didn't care anything about what I was learning. She wanted to hear about my cooking partner.

"Well, Corey finally paid

me a compliment. Sort of. He said I'd make a good chef, but that I needed to learn how to cook first."

Karyn laughed. "Some compliment. He sounds stuck up to me."

"Corey's not stuck up," I said. "I think he's just shy."

She rolled over onto her stomach, peering at me across the top of her sunglasses. "You like him!"

"No, I didn't say that—"

"You *do*! I can't believe it! A couple of weeks ago you told me your cooking partner was obnoxious."

"Well, a couple of weeks ago he was." I began to smile, but Karyn was giving me that Oprah look again. The one that said I had some sort of problem that needed solving immediately. "What?" I asked.

"Are you only interested in this guy because your mom is dating somebody?"

I laughed. "They only went out once, Karyn. One time. And Mom decided that Brent wasn't the guy."

"Did she decide that, or did you?"

I thought about that. "We both did."

"Uh-huh." Then Karyn gave me the look again.

I didn't feel like arguing with her. "Okay," I admitted. "I do sort of like Corey. And Mom and I are going over to his aunt's house later this week to look at some of her puppies."

"Puppies!" Karyn sat straight up. "Your mom's going to let you get another dog?"

"Maybe. We're just taking a look. But I'm hoping I'll find one she can't say no to."

"I wish I could get a dog." Karyn pouted. "But the apartment manager here won't allow us to have pets."

"How about this? If we bring home a puppy, I'll let you come over and play with him anytime you want. And Mrs. Hamilton might get a cat. You could play with her new kitten too."

Karyn made a face. "That mean old lady from next door?"

Was Mrs. H truly *mean*? I sure used to think so. Now I knew that she was just lonely. Mrs. Hamilton missed Millie, and she was angry that her cat had died. Maybe she was angry that her husband had died too. Face it. Losing things you loved was hard. I should know. I'd lost my father and my dog all on the same afternoon. But I could still see them whenever

I wanted to. What would it be like if they were really gone forever?

"I think Mrs. Hamilton only pretends to be mean so that she won't have to get close to anybody." Karyn leaned forward in her lounge chair, clearly interested. This was real *Oprah* stuff. Maybe even *Dr. Phil* material.

"Aaaah. Fear of attachment," she said, nodding her head, as if she had it all figured out. Hmmm. I decided that no matter how cranky my neighbor got, I'd try to stick by her. *And* find her a new pet. In the meantime, it was getting awfully hot out here. Time to cool off.

We both headed for the diving board.

Week number six in Shanti's class. Corey was busy at work in the cooking station, chopping an onion. A blender stood off to one side.

"What are we making today?" I asked.

"Shanti's Magical Quiche," he replied, and I laughed. "No, really. That's what she calls it. The crust forms on top instead of being on the bottom. It's great! I've been making this stuff since I was a little kid."

I glanced at the recipe, then began pouring milk into the blender. "Do your parents enjoy your cooking?" I asked, wondering if his father was as finicky about food as mine.

"Are you kidding? My mom's just glad she doesn't have to do it."

"Sounds like my mom," I said. "What about your dad?"

Corey looked at me before returning to his mound of onion slices. "He thinks it's dumb."

"Really?" I shredded some cheese. Okay, so my father wasn't continually gushing with compliments, but at least he had always encouraged me. He knew how much I loved to cook. So did Mom. Whenever they really wanted to punish me, they knew what to do. Banish me from the kitchen.

Corey pulled a package of bacon out of the small refrigerator and threw a few slabs into a frying pan. "My father thinks the photography stuff is dumb too."

That made me angry. "Well, what does he think *isn't* dumb?" I demanded.

I saw the faintest trace of a smile. "Football, baseball, and basketball," Corey said, tapping the words off on his fingertips. "And soccer, maybe."

"But your family should be supportive of what-ever you want to do," I said helplessly. "I mean, you're really good at cooking. And photography too. Aren't you?"

Corey shrugged. "You tell me."

"I will."

His mouth wrinkled up, and Corey turned his back on me. At first I thought he was ignoring me, but then I saw he was digging something out of his backpack. It was a photograph.

"I'm going to enter this in the photography ex-hibit at the museum next month," he said quietly, as if he didn't want anyone else to overhear.

I examined the photo. It was a black-and-white portrait of a large, happy-looking dog. The animal's eyes were shiny, and its tail was caught in midair, tiny wisps of hair sticking out sideways from it. The entire photograph told a story, but what was it? Com-plete joy, I thought. And pure love, the kind that only a dog can give you.

"It's wonderful," I said. "Is this one of Shanti's dogs?"

"It's Trooper, the dog with cancer," Corey replied. "I'm calling the picture *Salvation*."

"Why did you decide to do it in black-and-white?" I asked.

He pointed to Trooper's nose and the tips of black on his ears. "To show the contrasts," he said. "In color, Trooper is just caramels and browns. This is a lot more dramatic."

I could tell that Corey had really thought about this picture. And I wondered if his family had even seen it. "What do your parents think about it?"

He carefully returned the photograph to his backpack before answering. "They don't know anything about it," he said. "If the picture is chosen for the exhibit, maybe then I'll show it to them."

A test, I thought. To see if he was really good enough. Kind of like the "sample" of Shanti's cooking that my father wanted to taste when this class was finished. *Nearly perfect,* Dad had said. Wouldn't life be a lot easier if all the people in the world were like Trooper? Just wagging their tails and loving everybody?

"I bet you've shown it to your aunt, though, haven't you?"

He shook his head. "I want to surprise her," he said.

"Surprise me how?" Shanti had loomed up behind

him, like a dark cloud. As usual, those ears of hers hadn't missed a thing.

Corey shot me a look of panic, so I answered for him. "We thought we would add some cinnamon to the recipe," I said quickly. "You know, just to shake things up a bit."

She placed one slender finger against her lips, as if tasting the cinnamon in her mind. "That might work," she said. Then she drifted off to station four without another word.

Corey laughed. "Can you just imagine her face if she sees Trooper looking back at her from that exhibit?"

"*When* she sees Trooper, not *if*," I said. "It really is a great picture, Corey."

He removed the bacon from the frying pan and set it onto a paper towel. My cooking partner was trying hard not to appear smug, but his pride shone through. Corey stood a little taller, and his bony shoulders were pointed straight up and back.

"Cinnamon?" he finally said. "In a bacon-and-cheese quiche?"

I laughed. "Well, I didn't hear you coming up with anything better!"

He shook his head. "Thanks a lot, Evie."

Was he thanking me for covering for him? Or for liking his photograph? Did it really matter?

"It was nothing," I said.

But he knew what I really meant.

Shanti's Magical Quiche

½ pound bacon, cooked crisp and crumbled
1 cup shredded Swiss cheese
½ cup finely chopped onion
1 (11-ounce) can whole kernel corn with
    peppers, drained
2 cups milk
½ cup all-purpose flour
1 teaspoon baking powder
1 teaspoon sugar
4 eggs
½ teaspoon salt
¼ teaspoon ground black pepper

Preheat oven to 350 degrees F. and grease a 9-inch pie pan. Combine bacon, cheese, onion, and corn in the prepared pan. Place remaining ingredients in blender. Blend on high speed for 1 minute. Pour this mixture over bacon mixture in pan. Bake for 50 to 55 minutes. Let stand 5 minutes before cutting. Serves 8 to 10.

Evie's Kitchen Tip #12

To chop onions without crying, hold peeled onions under water as you cut them.

CHAPTER 13

Moderation

*"Too much of any herb can overwhelm
a food and make it bitter."*
—Betty Crocker

Mom backed our car out of the driveway. "Do you have any idea where we're going, Evie?" she asked.

"Shanti gave me directions to her house," I said, hoping that I remembered them. Now that I'd talked Mom and Mrs. H into taking this journey, I didn't want us to get lost somewhere out in the country.

Mrs. Hamilton asked me to navigate. She sat stiffly in the backseat, staring out the window. Mrs. H seemed uneasy, I thought. Maybe I shouldn't have pushed her into this so soon. I mean, she had barely gotten used to not having a cat around. Seeing all Shanti's pets might bring back too many hurtful memories.

Mom drove slowly around the block, avoiding the corner where she and I had found Millie over a month ago. But Mrs. H didn't seem to notice where we were going—or not going. She was lost in another one of her daydreams. I hoped it was a nice one, filled with lots of ornery cats.

Soon after we turned onto Route 92, I saw the white house to our left. Mom's car bumped along between overhanging oak trees until we pulled into a gravelly driveway already occupied by four other cars. Mom parked next to Shanti's daisy-covered van.

"Now, that takes me back!" she said with a booming laugh. I wanted to ask her back to *where*, but a barking dog cut me off. It was like a signal, I guess, because another dog began barking, then another and another.

Suddenly, an orange cat shot out through the front door and bounded noisily over the hood of our car. Mrs. Hamilton's hands flew to cover both ears, her face all scrunched up like crumpled newspaper.

Shanti exited next, all high spirits and swirly skirts. She approached the car, kicking up gravel with her worn leather sandals. Corey followed behind her, his hands shoved deep into the pockets of his jeans.

"Evie!" Shanti cried. "I'm so glad you made it. And this must be your mother."

Mom got out of the car to greet her. Mrs. H didn't budge.

Corey joined us, and Shanti introduced him. Then we all turned to stare at the car's sole occupant.

"Ummm, this is Mrs. Hamilton, my next-door neighbor," I said, hoping that my introduction might prompt the woman to get out of the car. It didn't.

Shanti popped her head through the rear window. "Good afternoon, Mrs. Hamilton," she said, her voice smooth and soothing. "Would you like to come in and see the menagerie?"

Mrs. H removed her hands from her ears. "Too noisy," she snapped.

At this, Shanti chortled heartily. "Oh, that. Don't let it bother you. The dogs will calm down in a few minutes. They just aren't used to this much company. Come on in."

She opened the back door of the car, and, to my relief, Mrs. Hamilton got out, glancing around as if expecting a rabid animal to attack her at any moment. She followed Shanti and my mother to the front porch.

"I'll let it bother me, if I want," Mrs. H muttered under her breath, as Corey and I came up behind her. We tried not to snicker.

I could see a maze of kennels and dog trails off to the left and was surprised at the size of Shanti's shelter. I had figured she might have a few dogs and cats, but nothing like this!

"Welcome to Furville," Corey said, and I laughed.

As we approached the front door, Shanti was greeted by more barks and squawks. A giant green parrot sat on a perch by the window, and three or four dogs were so eager for attention that they pressed against our legs, nearly knocking us over.

"The new puppies are in the backyard," Corey said, "*if* you can make your way out there, through all these dogs."

My mother grinned. Mrs. Hamilton stood, terrified, both elbows glued to her sides.

"Oh, here's a great big sweetie!" Mom's hand was getting licked by a large caramel-colored dog with deep molasses eyes. I recognized him immediately from Corey's photograph.

"This is Trooper," Shanti informed us, and for the first time Mrs. H actually moved one of her arms to reach down and pet the animal.

"Isn't he the sick one?" she asked, her voice raspy.

"Yes," Shanti said. "But I think Trooper can beat this. Chinese herbs, alternative treatments, music therapy. I will do whatever it takes."

"She's not kidding," Corey said. "My aunt feeds her animals herbs and supplements. And she cooks up all this smelly stuff with boiled fish and liver." He shivered in disgust.

Shanti smiled. "It's true," she said. "I use aromatherapy as well. Eucalyptus for healing, lavender for soothing, and peppermint to lift the spirits."

"Does any of it work?" Mrs. Hamilton asked skeptically. She was still petting Trooper's head.

"Sometimes," Shanti said. "And that's better than never."

The orange cat wandered back inside through Shanti's front door. In a great show of ignoring us, she hoisted her tail straight up in the air, like a flagpole.

"That's Desdemona," Shanti said, shaking her bracelets in the cat's direction. "She pretty much has the run of this place."

Trooper bristled at the sight of the orange cat, a deep gurgle rumbling in his throat. Desdemona glared back at him, frozen. Every hair on her body stood at attention. Then she suddenly attacked, landing on Trooper's back as the poor dog let out a howl.

Mom and I jumped. Mrs. H screamed. Shanti, meanwhile, calmly gave the cat a swat, and Desdemona sped off, disappearing down a dark hallway.

"Is that cat sick too?" I asked.

"No." Shanti laughed. "Just mean. If you're lucky, you'll see one of her kittens. They're hiding all over the house. Desdemona might seem vicious, but she's just being protective."

Shanti led us out back, where we saw a group of people gathered around a large enclosed structure. Inside was a mother dog who appeared to be asleep, and curled around her were half a dozen tiny creatures no bigger than tennis balls.

"Meet Maggie," Shanti said, "proud new mother."

The dog awoke and yawned, clearly uninterested in all these strange humans gawking at her. Maggie had more important things to worry about. Six of them, to be exact.

"She's so gentle," my mother said, melting. "What a sweet face for such a big dog. What kind is she?"

"A mix," Shanti said. "But there's plenty of Labrador in there, for sure."

"Will all her puppies get this big?" Mom asked nervously.

"Probably," Shanti replied. "Except for that one maybe." She was pointing to the far left, at the little one who was crawling over his brothers and sisters and making soft mewling sounds—almost like a kitten. "He's the runt, but what he lacks in size he makes up for in noise."

"Corey told me he might be blind," I said. "Is that true?"

She sighed. "Not totally blind, but I don't think he can see as well as the others. As a result, they keep shoving him out of the way and he's not getting very much of Maggie's milk. I have to supplement at least once a day with a baby bottle."

Mrs. Hamilton's voice was almost a whisper. "He's having a hard time."

We all watched the little dog rooting around in a circle. Occasionally, the other puppies would kick at him with their paws or butt him with their heads. I thought they were being awfully greedy.

Then one of Shanti's visitors spoke up. "I'd like that one in the middle, Shanti. The black-and-white puppy. When do you think they'll be ready to leave their mother?"

"In about three weeks," Shanti answered. "I'll mark you down for that one."

"Could I have the one with the white spot on his

back?" asked a woman in a yellow T-shirt that said PUPPY POWER.

"And I'd like the female, that puppy with the two white paws," added a man in a blue baseball cap.

I glanced anxiously at my mother. All the dogs were getting snapped up. What should we do? If I didn't say something now, I'd lose my puppy forever. *If* she'd consent to letting me have one.

Then Mom surprised me. "I want the solid black one!" she cried, before I could do more than open my mouth. But that was not the puppy I would have picked. I preferred the one with the wiggly pink nose. In fact, I had already chosen a name for him, in my head: Pinky.

"That fellow with the pinkish nose is quite handsome, isn't he, Evie?" Mrs. Hamilton said, as if reading my mind. I shrugged, pretending not to care. Why get attached to a dog who would probably be snatched up by tomorrow? Besides, if I objected to my mother's choice, she would probably be angry. Or hurt. Mom had her heart set on the black puppy now. And I was the one who had dragged her here, after all.

As we made our way back through the house, I spotted a black-and-orange kitten, its tiny whiskers poking out from beneath a couch cushion. The cat actually had one black ear, I noticed. Exactly like Millie! I saw Mrs. Hamilton hesitate, as if she'd just encountered a ghost. But then she walked on by, pretending she hadn't seen the cat at all.

"Are any of Desdemona's kittens available?" I asked, hoping that Mrs. H was listening for Shanti's answer.

"All of them," Shanti replied. "If you can catch one."

She led us to the door, inviting us to return any-time we liked. "You can come back for your new puppy in a month, Evie. I'm so glad you picked her."

Her! The puppy was a *her?* I didn't want a girl. I wanted a boy, like Mousse. And I didn't pick that puppy, either. Or hadn't Shanti even noticed?

As we climbed into the car, Corey pointed to Mrs. Hamilton and whispered, "I guess this didn't work out as planned, huh?" Yeah, right. If he only knew. "Well, I'll see you on Monday, Evie."

I sat in the back, resting my head against the seat. This trip was a total failure. Mrs. Hamilton had completely ignored the kitten, and my mother ended up adopting a dog I didn't choose.

"Wasn't that black puppy the cutest thing you ever

saw?" Mom gushed, starting up the car. Neither Mrs. Hamilton nor I responded, but my mother was on a roll. "And so black, like a little lump of coal. Black as midnight. That's it! We can call her Midnight! What do you think, Evie? Isn't that a perfect name?"

"Sure," I said. Why argue with her? You couldn't name a black dog Pinky. Besides, I could already see that Midnight—or whatever her name turned out to be—was destined to become my mother's dog.

We turned quiet then. The sun was going down, and Mom was trying to find her way back to Route 92 in the graying twilight. I peered out the passenger side as we rolled past dark, hulking trees and an occasional farmhouse with glowing windows. No one spoke until we were heading south on County Road 510.

"That woman looked familiar," Mrs. H said. "Haven't I seen her on television or something?"

"She's Betty Brightman," I said. "Or she used to be, anyway."

"You mean the lady who cooks with puppets?"

I nodded, although I didn't think Mrs. H could see my response in the fading light.

"How does she stand it?"

For a moment I thought Mrs. Hamilton was referring to the puppets. "Stand what?" I asked.

"Seeing all those dogs and cats, dying and disappointed. People walking away and leaving them. It
makes me angry when I see an animal that's hurt or
lonely."

"But Shanti treats them, and a lot of her animals
get better," I said.

Mrs. H snorted. "With what? Eucalyptus oil?"

I laid my head back on the seat again. I didn't want
to argue with her.

"Do you think she'll have that little blind one put
to sleep?" Mrs. Hamilton asked after a few minutes.
She didn't sound angry anymore, only sad.

Mom answered immediately. "Absolutely not.
Shanti doesn't believe in it. She *saves* animals that
are going to be put down."

"Well, there's that, I suppose," Mrs. H said.

No one talked for the rest of the ride home.

Evie's Powdered Sugar Brownies

½ cup (1 stick) butter
3 squares unsweetened chocolate
3 eggs
1½ cups sugar
½ cup flour
Dash salt
1 teaspoon vanilla
Powdered sugar

🍬 Preheat oven to 300 degrees F. and grease an 8-inch square baking dish. Line bottom of dish with waxed paper.

🍬 Combine butter and chocolate over low heat or melt at low microwave setting. Beat eggs until thick and foamy.

Then beat sugar into eggs thoroughly. Blend in flour. Add vanilla, salt, and chocolate mixture. Beat well.

🍂 Pour brownie batter into dish; bake for 45 minutes. Brownies will be sticky and look underdone. Turn out immediately onto a fresh sheet of waxed paper. Take paper off bottom of brownies and cut while hot. They will tear slightly.

🍂 When cool, roll in powdered sugar. Makes 2 dozen small brownies.

Evie's Kitchen Tip #13
Chocolate has some nutritional benefits for humans. But beware: It contains a chemical called theobromine that can be poisonous to dogs!

CHAPTER 14

Collaboration

"Never say no to offers of help."
—Tamara Weiss

From the end of the street, I could just make out the shape of my father's silver Corvette parked in the driveway. I'd expected our house to be closed and dark, but all the lights were on.

"I wonder why—" my mother began, pulling in as the front door opened and Mousse came bounding up to us, his tail thrashing back and forth like a riled-up snake.

"Hey, fella!" I jumped out and hugged him hard, thinking about Shanti's puppy with the pink nose.

Hard to believe that Mousse had been as small as that once.

Dad appeared in the doorway, bleary-eyed and unshaven. He looked as if he'd slept in his clothes.

"The babies are here," he said helplessly, waving an arm in Mousse's direction. "I didn't know what else to do with him."

Mom looked at Mousse, then at Dad. "Is Angie all right?" She finally asked.

Dad stared at her, clearly exhausted. "Angie's fine. She did great. And the babies are tiny. Five weeks early, but... great. A girl and a boy." My father seemed stunned, almost in shock, as if he couldn't really believe this was happening to him. Mousse, somehow sensing Dad's mood, ran around his legs in circles, barking noisily.

Mrs. Hamilton made her way over to the rest of us. "What babies?"

Then my mom, completely to my surprise, took two steps forward and wrapped her arms around my father's shoulders, patting him awkwardly on the back.

"We'll be happy to watch Mousse," she said. "*You* need to get yourself back to the hospital."

Dad nodded, then hurried to his car, started the engine, and drove away. Just like that. Not a word to me.

"What babies?" Mrs. H asked again in confusion.

"Ask my father!" I said, running inside and straight up to my room, before she or my mother could see my face. I locked the door and threw my body onto the bed, surrendering myself to a good hard cry.

I think I slept, because the room was dark with shadows when I heard a knock on the door. One glimpse at the clock beside my bed told me that I'd been moping in here for over an hour. I was suddenly embarrassed about the way I'd stormed into the house. And I especially regretted the way I'd snapped at Mrs. Hamilton. She couldn't help it if my father had decided to start a whole new family. Neither could my mother, when it came to that, but she didn't have to go and hug him.

"Please go away," I said, as politely as I could. "I want to be alone."

The tapping continued, and it didn't stop. *Tap . . . tap . . . tap . . . tap . . . tap.* Like Morse code on wood. It was really beginning to get on my nerves. Finally, I scooted off the bed, tiptoed to the door, and unlocked it. Then I scurried back and hid under the covers.

I heard the knob turn, and the door opened a crack.

"Evie?"

I peeked out from under my blanket, pretending I wasn't interested. The door swung wider, and a tiny white Kleenex appeared in the crack and began to wave up and down. In spite of myself, I let out a giggle.

Mom's head poked around the edge of the door.

"Just because I'm laughing, doesn't mean I'm happy, Mom," I warned her.

She continued waving her tissue. "Truce?" she asked.

Throwing back my covers, I sat up. In a way, I was actually relieved that my snit could now be over. I was tired of being angry. And I was tired of being alone in my room.

"Okay," I said.

Mom walked over to me. She carried a large red book under one arm. Mousse bounced in after her and jumped up on the bed. When he finally settled down, the mattress sort of sank in the middle, as if he'd burrowed a hole there for himself. Mom sat too, and rubbed the back of my hand.

I studied her long, piano-playing fingers. I remembered those fingers at my school carnival when I was only seven years old. They'd peeled the ends off a Band-Aid and covered my skinned knee when I fell down during the PTA Cake Walk. Those same fingers had pulled bubblegum out of my hair three years ago. And they probably changed countless diapers when I was too young to be aware of it. But thinking of diapers only reminded me of Dad's new twins, and I started blubbering again. Mousse hovered, whining protectively.

Mom reached out and smoothed the hair off my forehead. "It's hard to share him, isn't it?"

"Who?" I asked, thinking at first that she meant Mousse.

"Your father."

My throat ached, as if I'd been squeezed into a very small space with no air to breathe. I realized that this had to be hard for Mom too. Maybe harder than it was for me.

"Aren't you angry?" I blurted.

"Yes," Mom answered truthfully, "but not because of the twins."

Mousse burrowed in closer to me. I waited for my mother to go on.

"Did you see his face?" Mom said. "David was so happy, Evie. Happier than I've seen him in a long time. And I'm angry because I can't make him happy like that. Not anymore."

She had called him David.

"Not anymore, Evie," Mom said again, firmly. "It's over. It was over with us long before your dad left." She sniffed. "I just didn't want to see it." Mom wagged a finger at me. "But it's not over with you," she added. "You are the one thing that makes him every bit as happy as those twins."

My mother switched on the bedside lamp, and we moved over to the futon. She showed me the book I'd seen her carrying earlier. "Your father put this photo album together when you were a baby. But I think it really belongs to you."

I examined the album with its faded red cover. My name was scrawled across the front, *Evelyn Marie Carson,* in Dad's bold familiar script. I was surprised to see how closely the writing resembled my own.

The first photograph was now a washed-out red and brown color, and it pictured a much younger Dad holding a bundled-up baby. The caption said *Evie Carson, three days old.* The next photograph was clearer. Mom was sitting in our kitchen, only the wallpaper was different. All yellow and  flowery. She was smiling down at the baby in her arms, the child's gaze glued to her mother's face as if trying to memorize all its features. *Evie, age four, and Carolyn.*

It felt strange, seeing myself as a baby. Strange, and good too. My mother seemed so happy, just the way my dad had looked in the previous photo. I wanted to jump back into the happy world of those photographs and stay there. Keep everything from changing.

"Will he make a new album now?" I asked. "For the twins?"

"Probably," Mom said.

I closed the album then, not ready to go through the rest of it yet.

"But that doesn't take anything away from this album, does it?" Mom asked. Her voice was a little shaky.

When I didn't answer, she went on. "These photos can never be replaced, Evie. And neither can you."

I squeezed my eyes shut, determined not to get weepy again.

"It's kind of like Mousse, isn't it?" Mom said. "A new dog can't replace him either. Because you still love him, whether he lives here or on the other side of Clermont Lake. Right?"

I sulked, answering her question with one of my own. "But you want that little black dog to live with us on *this* side, don't you?"

She blinked, confused. "Well, sure. You mean, you don't?"

I ran my hand over the red photo album. "Ummm...no. Actually, I wanted the puppy with the pink nose."

Mom's mouth opened slightly, then closed again. "Oh." She rubbed her hands together in her lap.

"Oh," she said again, before looking at me. "I'm so sorry, Evie. I really got carried away. Why didn't you say something?"

"I could see that you really liked Midnight," I answered.

My mother shifted uncomfortably. "Let me call Shanti and tell her we've changed our minds. Maybe you can still get the one with the pink nose."

"No, it's okay," I said, and I grabbed her hand before she could leave. Pinky or Midnight, what did it matter? Neither one of them was Mousse. Which was what Mom had been trying to tell me in the first place.

As if he knew what I was thinking, Mousse nuzzled me with his nose, seeking attention as usual. I caressed him and watched his tail doing a little happy dance.

My mother grinned and gave him a big squeeze. Then she hugged me too. "I just want you to cheer up, Evie," she said. "Could you maybe work on that for me?" She stood to leave and started toward the door.

"Mom!" I shouted after her, and she turned around. "Do you think we could put some family pictures back in the hallway? Just a few?"

She looked at me, astonished. Her jaw tightened, then relaxed. "Is the mirror really so ugly?"

"Hideous."

Mom shrugged. "Sure, let's see what we can do. I owe you that much. For choosing the black puppy, I mean."

I smiled, holding up her Kleenex. "You forgot this," I said.

Mom gave her head a toss. "I have a whole boxful."

After she left my room, I decided to leaf through the photos again. It was weird, seeing myself that small and helpless. Both my parents held me gingerly, as if they thought I might break at any moment, and I realized that neither one of them knew anything about how to care for a baby thirteen years ago. They were as young and anxious then as Angie was now.

I gave Mousse a nudge with a corner of the album. "Here," I said. "We can look at this together."

But he was already fast asleep.

My father called later that evening to thank me for watching Mousse. Dad must have taken a nap too, because now he sounded more exhilarated than exhausted.

"Your mother said Mousse could stay with you for a few more weeks. Is that all right?"

"Sure."

"Look," Dad said, after a long pause. "Would you like to keep him? On a more permanent basis, I mean?"

I swallowed hard, wishing he'd made that offer a year ago.

"It was wrong of me to take Mousse in the first place," Dad added. "I think I only did it to be—"

"Spiteful?" I offered, and Dad laughed nervously.

"Probably," he said. "But I would rather have taken you."

I blinked, feeling weepy again.

"So I'm trying to make things right," he went on. "Do you still want him?"

"No," I said, finding my voice. "I mean, I don't think I could keep Mousse now. Not here, anyway. Mom's getting a puppy, and it probably wouldn't work out."

"Your *mother* is getting a puppy?" Dad sounded surprised.

"It's a long story," I said, "but thanks for offering, Dad." Then I added, "How's Angie doing?"

"Pretty wiped out," he said. "She's sleeping right now."

"What about the twins?"

"Oh, they're sleeping too. Both of them are in Intensive Care until they're big enough to handle visitors. How about it? Would you like to come see them when they've gained a little weight?"

Would I? I had to admit that I was curious to get a look at them. Especially after seeing those cute little puppies this afternoon. I wondered if the babies would resemble that little me I'd seen in the red photo album.

"Okay. Maybe Mom can bring me over some afternoon," I said.

"That would be great, pumpkin seed. You can't believe how small they are. Two tiny little people, with all their fingers and toes!"

I thought about what Angie had said to me. *Two new little people that you don't even know.* Right. But I figured I'd get to know them soon enough. And I was surprised to discover that I might actually be looking forward to it.

"After all, they need to meet their big sister," Dad

said excitedly. "The twins are going to love you, Evie."

I still didn't consider myself a big sister, but I guess that's exactly what I was. I now had a little sister and brother. Wow. My family was growing more crowded by the minute.

"Did I tell you their names?" Dad asked, sounding so proud I thought he might burst.

"No, you didn't, Dad."

"We named them Julia and Graham. What do you think?"

Of course. I got the joke immediately. Julia Child, the famous chef, and Graham Kerr, known on television as the Galloping Gourmet. Only my father would choose to name his children after people who cooked for a living.

"I think their names are perfect, Dad."

And I really did.

Evie's Lemony PTA Cake-Walk Cake

3 cups sifted cake flour
2 teaspoons baking powder
½ teaspoon salt
1 cup butter, softened
2 cups granulated sugar
1¼ teaspoon vanilla
¼ teaspoon lemon oil
5 eggs
⅔ cup buttermilk
¼ cup finely shredded lemon peel
½ cup lemon juice
1½ cup chopped pecans, toasted

FOR GLAZE:
¼ cup granulated sugar
2 tablespoons lemon juice

🍂 Preheat oven to 350 degrees F. Grease and flour a 10-inch Bundt pan. Set pan aside.

🍂 In a medium bowl, combine cake flour, baking powder, and salt; set aside. In large bowl, beat butter with an electric mixer on high speed for 30 seconds. Beat in sugar, vanilla, and lemon oil until fluffy and light, about 4 minutes. Add eggs, one at a time, beating 30 seconds after each addition. Alternately add the flour mixture and buttermilk to the butter mixture, beating on low speed after each addition and starting and ending with flour, until combined. Stir in lemon peel and lemon juice. Stir in pecans. Spoon batter into prepared pan.

🍂 Bake for one hour, until toothpick inserted near center comes out clean and top springs back when touched lightly. Let cake stand for ten minutes to cool.

🍂 GLAZE: In a small saucepan, heat and stir the ¼ cup sugar and 2 tablespoons lemon juice until sugar dissolves. Invert cake onto wire rack set over a shallow baking pan. Poke holes in top of cake with toothpick. Spoon glaze over cake. Cool completely before cutting.

Evie's Kitchen Tip #14

To get the most juice out of a lemon, roll it on the counter, under your palm, for a full minute before cutting.

CHAPTER 15

Composition

"To cook great food,
you have to have great ingredients."
—Emeril Lagasse

I prepared Monterey chicken on Saturday evening. The sauce was a little thick, but my mother finished off an entire plateful without any complaints. Afterward, I slipped a small portion to Mousse and he seemed to enjoy it too. So, maybe Shanti's cooking class was having some beneficial effects.

This was almost like old times, I thought. Mousse grunting happily under the table while Mom and I ate. But I knew that the "old times" were gone for good. Mousse was merely on loan for a few weeks.

And now Dad had a second family, and Mom was about to adopt a new pet. Everything had changed, and in only a few weeks. Or maybe it had been changing all the time, and I'd simply been too busy to see it. Did anything ever stay the same? I wondered.

As I rose to throw away the empty milk carton, Mom interrupted my thoughts.

"I've enrolled in a class at the rec center myself," she said. "On Tuesday nights."

"Really?" Mousse jumped up on me, and I wagged a finger at him in warning. "What kind of class?"

My mother set both hands on the kitchen table, palms down. "Promise me you won't laugh?"

"Sure," I said uneasily.

"I'm going to start belly dancing."

The picture in my mind was simply too funny. Sort of like the old reruns of *I Dream of Jeannie* I watched on TV with my mom. Only this genie was wiggling around in sneakers and baggy sweatpants. "Belly dancing?" I managed to say, without laughing.

"Yes. My friend Alice is taking the class with me. We thought it might be good exercise."

I busied myself with Mousse. When you can't

think of anything else to do, you can always pet your dog. And it's also a good way to hide your face.

"All right," Mom said, hands on hips. "I know you're laughing at me, but this is something I really want to do."

"Then go for it, Mom," I said. "I think you and Alice will have fun."

The phone rang, and Mom immediately said, "It's for you," as she rose and began clearing plates from the table. Now, how had she known that?

"Hello, Evie?" It was Mrs. Hamilton. After I'd been so rude to her earlier, I was surprised she wanted to talk to me. "Could you come over here for a few minutes? There's something I'd like to discuss with you."

I agreed to meet with her in a half hour, after the dinner dishes were cleaned up. I intended to apologize for snapping at her yesterday, but I sure wished that I'd made some brownies or cookies to offer along with my apology.

As I approached her house empty-handed, I saw Mrs. Hamilton sitting on the front porch in her wooden rocking chair, enjoying the view. She waved her hand at the empty chair next to her. "Sit down, Evie. We can talk here."

I sat obediently.

"I know what you and your mother were trying to do the other day, taking me to that animal shack." To my relief, Mrs. Hamilton didn't sound angry or annoyed. Merely amused.

When I didn't reply, she continued. "And I appreciate the thought, Evie. I really do. But, you see, I had already decided not to get a new cat."

"But—"

She raised a hand. "Just hear me out, now."

I sighed and sat back in my chair.

"I didn't think another cat could ever replace Millie, but there was also a second reason." Mrs. H stopped rocking and leaned forward urgently. "I'm an old woman, Evie. And I'm not sure how long I'll be around to take care of an animal. It wouldn't be fair."

I hadn't considered her situation that way. Again,

I'd gone and assumed that things would never change, but of course they had to. Mrs. Hamilton couldn't go on living forever. And she knew that, even if I didn't.

I met Mrs. Hamilton's intense eyes, as she added, "But I think I've changed my mind now."

Happily, I said, "You mean you *do* want a cat?"

"Noooo," she said slowly. "But I might want a dog."

I was too astonished to respond.

"And this is why I needed to talk to you, Evie. I called your friend Shanti, and I have already spoken to your mother, but the final decision is yours. You see, I will only take a dog if I can be sure he will be cared for after I am . . . gone. And if that happens—no, *when* that happens—I think you would be the best person to have it."

Tears stung, and my nose began to itch. "I would love to have your dog," I croaked, through my tightened throat.

"I'm sure of that, Evie." Her voice was gentle. "But would you love having a blind one?"

I stared at her as I digested the words. Mrs. Hamilton wanted the little blind dog that no one else had claimed. I smiled. "You bet I would."

She smiled too. "At least this is one pet who won't run away. And I figured that he can be my ears, and I can be his eyes. A good trade-off, don't you think?"

"Are you sure you're not getting this dog because you're worried he might be put to sleep?"

"No, no," Mrs. H assured me. "Shanti told me she would never do that, but I'm worried about him anyway. The poor little guy has to fight just to stay alive." She rocked back gently. "The fight almost went out of me when feisty old Millie got herself hit by a car. But then I thought to myself, I'm still alive. For a little while longer, at least. And I'm still kicking." She hoisted a skinny leg into the air and I laughed.

Mrs. H chuckled too and then grew immediately serious. "Do you think he'll like it here, Evie?"

"I think he'll love it here," I replied.

Mrs. Hamilton's head turned, her gaze taking in the oak tree, with Millie's grave resting peacefully underneath it. "I think Millie would be very agreeable to this, don't you?"

I didn't say anything. I wasn't sure I could trust my voice.

So I just nodded yes.

On the last day of Shanti's cooking class I woke early, prepared to attack a new breakfast recipe that I'd discovered in a magazine. "Egg Cetera," as it was called, was an ordinary omelet with lots of extra stuff thrown in. In fact, the list of ingredients ended with a note from the author: "For flavor and variety, add even *more* ingredients."

I thought about my original family of three—four, if you counted Mousse. Simple and ordinary, like most families. But what was ordinary? And what did I know about most families anyway?

And now, whether I asked for it or not, a lot of extra stuff had been thrown into the family pan, sort of like the added ingredients in my "Egg Cetera" recipe. Now I had a stepmother, two newborn siblings, and a brand-new puppy arriving in a couple of weeks. Add Mrs. Hamilton and her little blind dog next door, and you had quite a brimming potful. Flavor and variety, like the magazine said. Well. Nothing stays simple, especially in the kitchen.

I showed the recipe to Shanti later that morning, and she tapped a finger to her temple. "Ingredients are the key," she agreed. "Otherwise, cooking is just food."

"That sounds like a quote from one of my dad's cookbooks," I said to Corey as Shanti whisked off to another station. We were preparing the crusts for our apple pies today, rolling and molding the pastry dough.

"Roll with light strokes, from the center out," Shanti had instructed us. "And lift the rolling pin each time you get to the outer edge. *Never* roll back and forth, or from the edges to the center."

Easy for her to say. My rolling pin kept sticking to the dough, and I was creating a gooey mess. Corey clucked next to me, like a disgruntled hen. Finally, he grabbed the rolling pin from me.

"Use waxed paper," he suggested, placing the dough between two sheets of the paper and moving his wooden pin lightly over the top sheet. Now, why hadn't Shanti suggested that in the first place?

Next we were instructed to fold the rolled pastry in half and transfer it to the pie plate, making sure that the fold was in the center. Mine obviously wasn't. When I unfolded it, the doughy crust fell off to one side. I pulled at the other edge, and the whole thing tore in two.

"Do *not* stretch the pastry," Shanti said from the

center of the room. Jeez! Maybe Corey had been right. His aunt really did have eyes and ears in the back of her head.

"I give up," I whispered to Corey. "Can't we just use the frozen stuff?"

He had finished his pie crust and was now adding the filling. "You don't have enough patience," he said. I watched him take over mine, but for some reason I wasn't angry with him. I was too busy noticing that his shirt was pale blue today, the same color as his eyes.

Shanti circled around then, showing us how to apply the top crust and crimp the edges. "Don't be afraid to use your hands," she said, then added to me, "I'm delighted that your neighbor is taking a puppy, Evie." The cooking master clapped her flour-covered fingers together with a soft *poof.*

Corey raised an eyebrow at me as he began brushing the top of his pie crust with beaten egg whites.

"I'm happy too," I told Shanti. "Mrs. H really needed a companion."

"We all need companionship," Shanti said earnestly. "'Friends and food,' that's my motto."

When she left, I said to Corey, "I thought her motto was 'A home for every animal, and an animal for every home.'"

His shoulders rose and fell. "Guess that was her motto last week." He placed our pies in the oven and set the timer. "I can't believe your neighbor actually wanted a puppy," Corey said, shaking his head. "She seemed terrified of those dogs the other day."

"Mrs. Hamilton chose the runt, the little blind one," I explained. "I think she felt sorry for him."

He considered this, then grabbed a towel to wipe down the counter. "Well," Corey began, his voice rising a little, "I guess today is our last official day as cooking partners."

Uh-oh. I'd been dreading this. How would I ever talk to Corey after today? I imagined myself making all sorts of excuses to call his house. *I'm all out of brown sugar. Do you have any measuring spoons?* Ugh! He'd see through my charade in a minute. Besides, I didn't even have his phone number.

"I could always e-mail you some of Shanti's recipes," Corey said then, and I wondered if maybe—just maybe—he might be thinking the same thing. Wondering how *he* could talk with *me*, I mean.

"Okay," I said. "But I'll probably find a way to ruin every one of them."

"You'll do fine, Evie," he said. "You're a good cook. Really."

"Thanks." I began washing the rolling pins, not sure what to do next. Corey continued to scour the countertop, but I noticed that his neck and ears were bright red.

"The photography exhibit opens at the museum in a couple of weeks," he said quickly. "And I entered the picture of Trooper. Wanna go?"

I scrubbed at those rolling pins until they were spotless. Was Corey asking me out on a date?

"I mean . . . do you want to go with *me*?" he added.

"You bet," I said, grinning at him, and not even caring how stupid I looked.

He let out a long breath, and then—thank God—the oven timer buzzed.

Evie's Monterey Chicken

2 boneless skinless chicken breasts
4 teaspoons barbecue sauce
4 slices very crisp bacon
½ cup grated Monterey Jack and cheddar
   cheese blend
salt and pepper
1 cup tomatoes, chopped
½ cup chives

🦴 Pound chicken breasts until somewhat flattened and season with salt and peper. In a nonstick skillet, cook chicken breasts until done (10 to 15 minutes). Transfer to baking sheet.

🐝 Top chicken breasts with barbecue sauce, bacon, and cheese. Broil chicken breasts in oven 3 to 5 minutes. Remove from oven and top with tomatoes and chives.

🐝 Serves two.

Evie's Kitchen Tip #15
Covered chicken takes longer to cook in the oven than uncovered chicken.

CHAPTER 16

Culmination

*"Sharing good food with friends and family
will make everybody a happier person."*
—Wolfgang Puck

"Hurry up, Mom!" I shouted. "Mrs. Hamilton is waiting for us."

Today, after weeks of waiting, we were finally driving to Shanti's place to officially adopt Midnight and Mrs. Hamilton's little blind puppy.

Dad and Angie were coming over later with the twins to collect Mousse. I would miss him, but I wasn't sure how he'd react to the puppies. One swat of Mousse's tail could send those two little dogs into orbit. So, maybe it was a good thing Dad was taking him back.

Mom appeared in the kitchen, holding a brand-new leash and a tiny collar. "I'm ready when you are," she said excitedly.

My mother drove faster than usual. And she hummed a tune as she accelerated, probably something fast and furious—like the "Minute Waltz." Mrs. Hamilton sat in the backseat again, ready to spring out the door. Good thing she couldn't actually see the speedometer.

"I think it's wonderful that you're taking the blind puppy," Shanti gushed as she helped Mrs. H out of the car. Corey stood behind her, grinning at me.

"Well," Mrs. Hamilton said, "I guess we'll both have to get used to each other. I've never owned a dog before."

Mom had already sprinted off across the driveway, and the rest of us scurried to catch up with her.

"What are you going to name him?" Corey asked Mrs. H as we made our way through his aunt's house and out to the backyard.

The old woman stopped at the door of the kennel, staring in at the little dog that was now hers. Then, gently, Mrs. Hamilton opened the door and placed her hand inside, underneath his nose. The dog sniffed at her and let out a loud bark, bumping his head against her arm.

"I think I'll call him Scrapper," Mrs. H announced firmly. "Because he's a good little fighter."

"And a noisy one too," Shanti added.

"Oh, I don't mind that," Mrs. Hamilton said seriously. "My hearing's not so good anyway."

Shanti placed the tiny dog in the woman's arms, and he tried to wriggle out of her grasp.

"I don't blame you, Scrapper," Mrs. H said. "You don't know me very well yet."

My mother held our little black puppy too as she made soft cooing sounds at her. The tiny dog was trembling in her arms. "Don't you worry, Midnight," Mom crooned. "Your brother is going to be living right next door."

We carried our dogs to the car and carefully climbed in. Scrapper's nose was taking in every scent, but he rested in Mrs. Hamilton's lap as if he'd been sitting there all his life.

Corey rushed to the car, carrying a couple of worn blue blankets. "Here," he said. "Shanti told me to give you these. The dogs have been sleeping on them, and she thought they might like to have something familiar to take to their new homes."

I rolled down the window and took the blankets for Mom and Mrs. Hamilton. Midnight wiggled anxiously in my lap as my mother started the car.

"Are we still on for tomorrow night?" I whispered. The photography exhibit had just opened at the museum.

He nodded. "Be prepared to do a lot of walking. There are over two hundred chosen entries this year."

"Is yours one of them?" I asked, holding my breath.

Corey held up both thumbs and beamed as Mom backed out of the driveway. I let out a whoop, and Midnight lifted her black nose as we picked up speed.

"I think your dog likes car rides, Mom," I said. Then I remembered that Mousse liked them too, and this made me a little sad.

The first thing I did when we arrived home was to set Midnight down in the backyard, so she could meet Mousse. Mrs. Hamilton followed me, carrying Scrapper.

Mousse ran up to us and Midnight stood perfectly still. She looked frightened, and alert. Mousse's ears sprang straight up, then he circled the intruder, sniffing.

"You'd better grab Midnight, Evie," Mom warned. "Mousse is about to maul her."

Suddenly, Scrapper jumped out of Mrs. Hamilton's arms, barking his fool head off. Mousse ran up to him, and Scrapper barked again. Midnight joined in, but Mousse put a paw out to graze her nose. Then Scrapper ducked his head and butted his shoulder against Mousse. Mousse leaped, bumping into Midnight, and all three dogs went down together, in a tangle of paws and tails. Scrapper righted himself first and barked at Mousse some more.

"Somebody stop them!" Mom shrieked, but I noticed that Mrs. H was smiling.

I stayed right where I was. "They're only playing, Mom."

My mother ran up to Mousse and tugged on his collar. "Come with me, you big bully," she said, dragging him away. I lifted Scrapper and handed him to Mrs. Hamilton, then scooped up Midnight, and we all went inside.

Once the dogs were in the house, the puppies

went over to Mousse's bowl of water near the kitchen sink. Mousse growled, ran over to the bowl, pushed both dogs aside, and started drinking noisily. Scrapper growled back at him, but stayed a respectful distance away.

"I think I'll take Scrapper home for a while," Mrs. H said anxiously. "He's had enough excitement for one day. And so have I."

After she left, I opened the cabinet under the sink and rummaged around until I found a little yellow bowl. Mousse had used that bowl a long time ago, and I'd never gotten rid of it. After filling the bowl with water, I set it down on the floor.

"Here you go, Midnight. This one's all yours."

The little black dog walked over and started to drink, as if she already knew she lived here. I guess Mousse knew it too, because he finished off his own bowl without glancing at Midnight again.

"I think it's time for Mousse to finally come home," I said to Dad four weeks later. He and Angie lumbered into their living room along with Mousse, two babies, two baby carriers, and two diaper bags.

Angie set Julia down and unfastened the safety

strap. Mousse jumped playfully against my father's legs, and Dad leaned down to give his dog a good hard hug.

I led Dad and Angie into the dining room, where I was setting out my very own snob dinner for August, in honor of Mousse's homecoming.

"Everything's here," I said. "Homemade quiche, red bean salad, and pineapple upside-down cake."

Angie sat down and let out a long sigh. "It all looks so wonderful, Evie," she said. "I haven't had a home-cooked meal in weeks."

I stared at Dad in amazement.

He shrugged apologetically. "No time to cook anymore, with two babies in the house."

Wow, I thought. Carson's Cuisine resorting to takeout? Wait until Mom heard about this latest development.

My father dug into Shanti's "Magical Quiche" and began to chew, while I held my breath. Angie winked at me from across the table, but I was too nervous to even smile back at her.

Oh, gulp. This was the final test. Many weeks of cooking with Shanti, and now Dad was sampling my finest efforts. Would he like this meal or not?

My father wiped his lips with a napkin and leaned way back in his chair. I reached under the table and grabbed a clump of Mousse's shaggy fur.

"Not bad, Evie," Dad finally said, placing the napkin back in his lap.

I stared at him. "Are you sure? It doesn't need any more salt or anything?"

"Nope."

"How about pepper? Or maybe some oregano?"

"Nothing. This quiche is nearly perfect, pumpkin seed. I like it just the way it is."

Nearly perfect. Dad actually thought my quiche was nearly perfect. And that was plenty good enough.

"Well, thank goodness for that proclamation!" Angie declared, cutting into the quiche for herself. "Does this mean *I* can have a piece now too?"

After I got home, I decided to drop in next door and check on Mrs. Hamilton and Scrapper. I also wanted to invite her over to sample some of my leftover pineapple dessert.

It was a clear night, bright with stars. The trees along the lake were black silhouettes, the moonlight making them appear taller than they ever looked in the daytime. I slowed to walk beneath the tree where Millie the cat lay, buried and at peace.

Over the past month I had traveled by this same patch of dirt and grass, with Mousse at my heels. It was strange now to be without him. I thought of the dreadful sadness I had felt when we buried Millie here, and now the similar sadness of giving Mousse up for a second time. And I thought about those old snapshots of me in the album Dad had assembled so long ago. And the photographs of my family in the hallway. My old family, the way it *used* to be.

Then I caught a glimpse of Mrs. Hamilton through the window. She was nuzzling Scrapper and whispering something to him. He raised his tiny head and licked her on the face, but not before delivering a little nip on her nose. I grew lighter inside.

I remembered something Shanti had told me about dogs and their masters. She'd heard that some Indian tribes believe that when you die, and it comes time to cross over into the spirit world, all the dogs you've ever owned in your life must hold on to a log with their teeth. And it is on this log that you must walk to safely enter the afterlife. Well. Mrs. H's journey would be a secure one, I thought. I knew for certain that her little blind dog possessed the teeth of twenty.

Quickening my pace, I stepped across Mrs. Hamilton's porch and knocked on the door.

Later, Karyn and Mrs. H came over. Karyn couldn't wait to get her hands on Midnight and Scrapper. All of us sat at the dining room table, munching happily. Then Mom brought in coffee for Mrs. H and some lemonade for Karyn and me.

"Where are the puppies now?" Karyn asked, and then she saw them, lying in the living room half hidden under their identical blue blankets.

"I believe they're really settling in," Mrs. H said, sounding pleased.

"They feel safe here, don't you think?" Mom asked. She was clearing the table, dressed in her old clothes, with no makeup on. And I liked her best this way. Just plain old Mom, without the purple eyelids. I hoped she would meet a man who liked her that way too—more than he liked his Lexus. But I didn't think I was quite ready for another of Mom's boyfriends just yet.

I pushed my chair back and stood, reaching for

the pineapple upside-down cake I'd prepared this morning, long before the sun had come up. The crust was slightly burnt around the edges, but Dad had polished off two nearly perfect pieces before sending me home with the leftovers, so I was pleased with my efforts.

Let's face it. I still wasn't a celebrity chef. Not yet, anyway. And I still couldn't keep Mousse here with me. But, at least I had family close by, to keep him *for* me. And to pretend that my cooking was magnificent, even when it sometimes wasn't.

I also had another date with Corey this weekend, and I couldn't wait. His photo had taken a third-place

ribbon in the museum exhibit, and he invited me to go with him to the awards ceremony on Saturday.

Oh, yeah. And speaking of photographs, Mom and I now have some old family photos hanging in our hallway too. Not a lot of them, but a few. My dad brought them over in a cardboard box yesterday.

And Corey helped me hang 'em.

Evie's Nearly Perfect Pineapple Upside-Down Cake

6 tablespoons butter, softened
⅓ cup packed brown sugar
½ cup water
1 (8-ounce) can pineapple slices,
   drained
4 maraschino cherries, halved
1⅓ cups all-purpose flour
⅔ cup granulated sugar
2 teaspoons baking powder
⅔ cup milk
1 egg
1 teaspoon vanilla

Preheat oven to 350 degrees F. Melt 2 tablespoons of the butter in a 9-by-1½-inch round baking pan. Stir in brown sugar and water. Arrange pineapple and cherries in rows, in the bottom of the pan. Set pan aside.

🍂 In a medium mixing bowl, stir together flour, granulated sugar, and baking powder. Add milk, the ¼ cup butter or margarine, egg, and vanilla. Beat with an electric mixer on low speed till combined. Beat on medium speed for 1 minute. Spoon batter into the prepared pan, being careful not to disturb the fruit arrangement.

🍂 Bake for 30 to 35 minutes. Let cool for 5 minutes. Loosen sides; turn cake upside down onto a plate. Serve warm or at room temperature.

🍂 Serves 6 to 8.

Evie's Kitchen Tip #16

You can make your own maraschino cherries by marinating pitted cherries in a solution of sugar, water, lemon, almond extract, and red food coloring.
Bon appétit!

Kitchen Wisdom from the Pros

Batali, Mario. *Mario Batali: Simple Italian Food*. New York: Clarkson Potter, 1998.

Beard, James. *James Beard's Simple Foods*. New York: John Wiley & Sons, Inc., 1993.

Betty Crocker, editors. *Betty Crocker's Cooking Basics: Learning to Cook with Confidence*. New York: Wiley Publishing, Inc., 2000.

Clark, Ann. *Quick Cuisine: Easy and Elegant Recipes for Every Occasion*. New York: Dutton, 1993.

Colicchio, Tom. *Think Like a Chef*. New York: Clarkson Potter, 2000.

Flay, Bobby. *Bobby Flay's Boy Meets Grill*. New York: Hyperion, 1999.

Florence, Tyler. *Tyler Florence's Real Kitchen*. New York: Clarkson Potter, 2003.

Garten, Ina. *The Barefoot Contessa Cookbook*. New York: Clarkson Potter, 1999.

Heloise. *In the Kitchen with Heloise*. New York: Perigee, 2000.

Lagasse, Emeril. *Emeril's TV Dinners*. New York: William Morrow, 1998.

———. *Prime Time Emeril*. New York: William Morrow, 2001.

Moulton, Sara. *Sara Moulton Cooks at Home*. New York: Broadway Books, 2002.

Puck, Wolfgang. *Live, Love, Eat! The Best of Wolfgang Puck*. New York: Random House, 2002.

Weiss, Tamara. *Potluck at Midnight Farm*. New York: Clarkson Potter, 2002.